T0036123

YOUR
SHADOW
HALF
REMAINS

S U N N Y
M O R A I N E

YOUR
SHADOW
HALF
REMAINS

NIGHTFIRE

TOR PUBLISHING GROUP
NEW YORK

YOUR SHADOW HALF REMAINS

Copyright © 2024 by Sunny Moraine

A Nightfire Book
Published by Tom Doherty Associates / Tor Publishing Group
120 Broadway
New York, NY 10271

www.tornightfire.com

Nightfire™ is a trademark of Macmillan Publishing Group, LLC.

The Library of Congress Cataloging-in-Publication Data is available upon request.

ISBN 978-1-250-89220-1 (trade paperback)
ISBN 978-1-250-89221-8 (ebook)

Our books may be purchased in bulk for promotional, educational, or business use. Please contact your local bookseller or the Macmillan Corporate and Premium Sales Department at 1-800-221-7945, extension 5442, or by email at MacmillanSpecialMarkets@macmillan.com.

First Edition: 2024

Printed in the United States of America

0 9 8 7 6 5 4 3 2 1

Here is the repeated image of the lover destroyed.
Crossed out.
Clumsy hands in a dark room. Crossed out. There is
    something underneath the floorboards.
Crossed out.

—RICHARD SIKEN

1

The sun is just beginning to scatter its light through the tops of the oaks when Riley throws her cell phone into the lake.

If asked, she wouldn't say she's given this decision a tremendous amount of thought. Standing there on the bank with her boots half-sunk in the mud, watching the spreading ripples where the phone went in, she realizes that it doesn't feel like a decision at all. It feels like the natural culmination of a long series of events, each gathering with the other into something with unstoppable inertia. Rolling down the days and weeks and months.

Didn't have a choice in it, she thinks, in the feeling of the solid little weight leaving her hand and the sound of it hitting the water with a soft *splosh*. It was just time.

Which of course gets her wondering about the last thing she really did have a choice in. She isn't sure what that would have been.

Riley shoves her hands into her pockets, tips her head back, and stares blankly up at the blue sky cutting through the network of branches and nodding leaves above her. Once in some long-forgotten and therefore likely forgettable piece of writing, she read that the sky was the face of

God. Bad poetry, that is. But if one granted that it was, in any respect, true, then where would God's eyes be located? Could she be looking into them without knowing it?

Then we could go insane and try to kill each other, she thinks, and the corner of her mouth twitches in what isn't remotely a smile. *I have a feeling that would probably only go one way.*

Or there is no God, which she's always found most plausible—even Before, let alone now.

The cell phone is gone. The world is further away now. She realizes, as she turns and heads back up the small slope to rejoin the path toward home, that she feels nothing whatsoever about it.

She doesn't feel as though she's lost anything at all.

One thing she could say about the cell phone is that it was very old. It was starting to work more slowly, and its operating system was losing stability. She would have had to replace it soon anyway—or the logic of Before would have declared as much. In any case, that would have been done easily enough; place an order online and then sit back and wait. Wait for probably a while, because it takes a long time for things to arrive in the mail now, and it seems as if it's taking longer every day. What once would have taken a week or so can now drag on for a month or more. Could be the mail itself, but it's just as likely to be on the production end.

They don't make anything like they used to. Many things being completely automated now has apparently made nothing better or more efficient. Once chip production faltered and then nearly collapsed, people began going back to the old items, the previously discarded items, and *functional* took almost universal precedence over *new*.

First, humans moved away from manufacturing and robots moved in. Then materials were harder and harder to come by, and so many robots sat idle, waiting for shipments that came late and irregularly or never came at all. And now so much less of everything is made.

These are the things Riley is meditating on as the house comes into view through the trees. It's a house somewhere in between—too large to be a cabin, yet somehow not quite what most people would consider a House. The siding is faded from blue to a dirty grayish white, and the roof is mossy; the place as a whole is old and not well maintained.

Riley is no expert at home maintenance. She might have taught herself, but she might have done any number of things. And then again, as with so much else, it's increasingly difficult to gauge the degree to which any given thing matters very much.

The gutters, leaf-choked. The flower beds around the sides of the house, badly in need of weeding. Starlings have nested in the chimney. As she makes her way down the gravel path toward the front porch, Riley notes these things as she always does: as the only markers of time's passage that hold any real weight anymore. They establish her presence, that she's been here. That she's here now.

She's found that if you don't see other people for long enough, you begin to lose hold of that. You come unmoored and begin to drift, often in ways you couldn't have predicted.

Her phone is sinking into lake mud. Possibly she's well and truly drifting.

The screen door squeak-clacks behind her, and she stands in a shaft of sunshine that cuts through the tiny front hall's gloom. She wipes her shoes on the ancient rug, and as she does, she notes—in the way she noted the gutters and the flower beds—the dark brown stains spattered in broad streaks and drops across the floorboards. Pooled against the scuffed white baseboard. Dripping down the faded green-and-gold floral wallpaper. There's a great deal of it. When a woman shoots her husband of forty-four years in the head and chest several times and then slits her own throat with a knife, it tends to be messy.

By the time Riley got the call—as the only surviving relative of her grandparents, there was no one else for authorities to contact—it wasn't even close to the first time she had to reckon with how much blood is in a human being, but it's still a bit of a sight to behold.

She might have properly taken care of the stains when she moved in, but again, she might have done any number of things.

Maybe that's part of the time thing, too.

She steps over the stains. Avoids them as best she can. Goes into the dim kitchen and makes herself a cup of tea. The kettle is electric, and therefore, with the frequent blackouts—more and more frequent, it seems—not always usable, but right now, the power is on. The tea is black and strong. She's running low. She'll have to order more very soon if she wants to wait only a month or so for it to arrive.

Although every time she places an order for anything, she half wonders if this will be the time it doesn't come at all.

As she sits at the kitchen table and sips her tea, she thinks about the phone in the mud beneath around ten feet of water. The mud, stirred gently by the water, will have already begun to entomb it, like a skeleton setting to fossilize. In hundreds of thousands of years, will someone find it?

Will there be anyone left to do the finding? Will anything have changed? Will people still be going mad when they meet one another's eyes, murdering, suiciding, or will it be over?

We're all under the water, she thinks. *I should jump in and join it*. Lie down in the mud. Pull it over like a soft, cold blanket.

She digs her thumbnail into the pitted tabletop so hard it splinters. At the same instant, she realizes she's been chewing her bottom lip so hard she tastes blood. She stops, feels a distant echo of unease. No, she moved out here so that she wouldn't kill herself. Or that's what she told herself at the time.

Time.

Which is the mud that covers.

Riley closes her eyes, swallows the tang of her own blood. In the trees outside, crows scream.

2

Crows scream.

Later, she would identify that as the tip-off. Maybe it was in direct response to what was happening out on the street and maybe it wasn't, but there was a harshly hysterical quality to the screaming that stood out to her and drew her to the apartment window. Drew her gaze down.

Two people were fighting in the street below.

Riley watched them, her head cocked birdlike.

She had seen street fights before. Or at any rate, she had seen fights in the street. Growing up in a neighborhood that she would have characterized as rough*ish* rather than rough, she saw more than her share of disputes settled with fists and clumsy grappling. It's a thing she learned from personal experience: fights are clumsy things. There's far more grabbing than punches or kicks. You spend more time on the ground than on your feet.

This was clumsy, too. But it wasn't like any fight she'd ever seen, and the first thing that struck her was how much blood there was, because one of the two people appeared to be fighting with their teeth.

He lunged and snapped at the air. Two stories up, she

could see the whites of his rolling eyes. Red streamed down his chin, gleamed in smoggy afternoon sunlight. He grabbed the woman he was fighting, yes, and he did so to hold her in place long enough to take a chunk out of her upper arm.

The woman scrambled to her feet. Tried to run. Tripped over nothing and went down, and he was on her again. By then, there was a small crowd. Stopped cars, honking. Raised cell phones. A general air of confusion. If it were a normal fight, Riley thought later, probably someone would have tried to break it up. Maybe. Most likely. But no one did. They stared and filmed, and the man tore the woman's throat out. A hot dog vendor across the street stood there, jaw slack, as the dog in the bun he was holding slipped free and fell into the gutter. An elderly man gripped a parking meter and vomited all over his shoes. A girl who couldn't have been more than sixteen burst into a peal of frightened giggles. The honking had stopped by then, or at least it seemed to have faded, and the street was eerily quiet.

Why did she notice those details? Why did her mind decide they were worthy of retention? The man was chewing a strip of flesh, diving back in for more. The woman was choking up her own blood, her feet twitching. Riley realized that she had one hand pressed against her mouth, the other jammed against the window sash. She wondered if she was screaming. She had never seen anyone die before.

She saw lots of people die after that.

Maybe that was Patient Zero. Maybe it wasn't. It's never been conclusively determined. All they know is that it didn't happen all at once, until it was happening everywhere. As it turns out, for no apparent reason, something can break in your world, and suddenly, all around you, people are dying bloody and screaming every fucking day.

It's horrifying. Then it's weird. Then it's inconvenient.

Then it's just every fucking day.

3

She does have a desktop computer with an internet connection—of sorts. It's satellite, not fiber-optic; she learned early on that with satellite, outages are less frequent. They do still happen, though, and every time she boots the thing up, it's a wild guess as to whether her one connection to the world beyond this property will be there.

It's there this time. She checks her email. She does this only to establish whether her latest order of food has shipped. It has; if all goes well, it'll arrive before she starts to run low of too many items. Unless the production end has also finally broken down, if no one is left to maintain the automation and the drones.

Vast fields devoid of human hands. All metal and wires and quiet whirring. Sometimes she sees it in her dreams. It's a safe thing to see.

There are a few other unread messages. She doesn't read them. She barely registers what they are before she kicks the thing into sleep mode, and she promptly forgets them. This is such a deeply ingrained mechanism at this point that she's barely aware that she does it.

A mechanism of what kind? Coping? Or something else?

If she were inclined to think about it at all, she would wonder why the fuck it matters anymore, whether it ever did.

What does coping even mean? She's alive, she isn't freezing or starving; as such, her life is reasonably comfortable. She's managed to avoid looking directly at human eyes, physically present or in an image, for over two years. Isn't this enough?

But she won't ask that question, because there's no reason to.

She wants to wash her face and lie down. In the bathroom, she stares at the blank wall where the mirror used to be. There are no mirrors anywhere in the house. Every surface capable of any significant reflection has been covered or removed or smashed. Last time she checked—which was, in fairness, a very long time ago—there was no clear evidence that meeting your own reflected gaze was sufficient to trigger a reaction, but why take chances?

Lying in bed staring at the shadows gathering on the ceiling, tracing her fingertips slowly over her own features like that old stupid cliché of a blind person learning someone's face. Her touch is incurious, absent. It creates no image in her mind. She doesn't need to see herself. It's not as if anyone else is seeing her.

4

At first, no one knew what the rules were.

This is a thing she remembers with visceral clarity, a kind of distant but gut-twisting sense memory. Even when people began to figure out that it was a look that triggered it, and before the terror of how common and mundane and borderline unavoidable such a thing was truly settled in: there was the terror of not knowing *what made it happen,* what was safe and what was hazardous and what was for-sure deadly, what would kill you and whoever had the misfortune to encounter you before you killed yourself.

But the rules came later. It took a few days for people to fully grasp that anything big was even happening.

Geographically widespread, temporally diffuse disasters are emergent phenomena. They lack the clarity of the singular event that happens all at once and right out in the open, spectacular and undeniable. People wonder and doubt. People conspiratorialize. Hoax, a lot of people said. Or fake news or false flag, and many of them continued to use those words even as people they personally knew went insane and destroyed the people around them and destroyed themselves.

So here, here is Riley in those first few days: in bed and on her couch and on her floor and nowhere in particular, with a face she no longer clearly sees, scrolling and scrolling and scrolling as if she can reach an informational saturation point at which she'll finally understand what's happening. She had caved to that impulse before—of course, everyone had—but this felt wholly different, because it was.

Platforms did what they could to crack down on imagery, on video; moderators struggled to delete them as soon as they were posted. But it proved impossible to keep up. It was a torrent, and it grew heavier all the time—of screams, of blood, of crushed bone, of torn flesh, of cars ramming through crowds and into buildings, of gunfire, of flashing knives, of any weapon anyone could get their hands immediately around.

Anything might become a weapon. In the midst of their insanity, this new form of *infected* proved amazingly resourceful. Creative, even.

But the violence is so easily made abstract. It's easier to look at, because it's numbing and because it's filtered through a screen, and Riley did not and does not have to think about the fear grinding into her stomach—how she could hide from it. How she could make herself safe.

Now there is no fear, but then, there was, ubiquitous as the screams.

She called out of work. Everyone was doing that by then. For days, she only ordered delivery, instructed them to leave it outside the apartment door. She saw no one, spoke only to her mother—a frantic voice high and tinny through the phone, *Oh god, honey, today Mark Hanlon across the street, you remember him, he let you use his pool, he killed the postal carrier with a shovel, the police had to shoot him, please stay away from everyone, please just stay inside.*

Riley said nothing. Only listened. Staring at the shadows on the ceiling, noting how they seemed to join with a couple of water spots to form a ghostly face.

A day later, it started showing up, text in the gaps between the images. Spreading as such things do, both weighty and questionable, unofficial but with such a ring of truth if for no other reason than that it's information at all.

But she immediately knew it was true. She knew it because part of her had known it already.

It's in the eyes.

5

Riley does leave the property in the most technical sense. But this area is sparsely populated, scattered vacation chalets ringed around the lake, and mostly woods in between. She knows some of those houses are empty now. Maybe most of them. She isn't certain. She doesn't go near them. Now and then, across water gone dark glass with evening, she sees the flicker of a light. But it never lasts.

She walks in the woods, and that's about it.

But periodically, she does go down to the road, to pick up mail or other deliveries, and also sometimes it's simply a thing she does. Down the long gravel drive to the winding ribbon of asphalt, and she always looks at it for a moment or two, as if reaffirming to herself that it's there.

Occasionally she catches the whirring insectoid form of the drone rising over the trees, hears its hum.

Today she's going, boots crunching rhythmically over the gravel. Dappled light across the gray fades in and out as clouds skate across the face of the sun. The drive rounds a bend, and the barred metal gate and the road come into view, and also several boxes piled neatly by the mailbox. She feels a flush of pleasure at the unexpected. Her food order, for once here much faster than she'd thought it would be.

She pays extra for more rapid and consistent deliveries. The money her mother and grandparents left her is sufficient for that, given how low her other expenses are, even with the wild swings in prices, which have become the norm as the economy staggers drunkenly along—although she's aware that eventually the money will run out, and government assistance may or may not be enough if it even exists at all by then. But even with the rapid delivery premium, her orders are arriving less regularly all the time.

Take what comes to you when it comes, be glad it came, and try to not dwell uselessly on the self-evident truth that while civilization didn't collapse totally and immediately the way one might have expected, everything is slowly, inexorably falling apart.

She unlatches the gate and creaks it open, crouches by the boxes and looks them over, notes with additional pleasure that they haven't been banged up too severely and probably nothing will be busted or broken open.

Something moves in the upper periphery of her vision and she jumps slightly, and in a twitch of reflex, her gaze shifts from the stack of boxes to a pair of shoes.

It stops there for what feels like a long moment. She sees only her own shoes these days. It's incongruous to encounter a pair that are not hers—chunky hiking boots—and on someone else's feet. Slowly upward: ankles and a glimpse of gray sock, legs enclosed by jeans, knees, upper thighs.

At the slim brown belt, she jerks her focus back to the

ground. Not even the boots are safe. The boots invite further investigation.

"Hi."

Low, pleasant voice. Riley's mind snags on processing that as well. A voice that isn't hers. A voice that isn't recorded audio (without imagery, always without imagery). Real-time and present and in proximity.

"It's all right," says the voice. "I put blinders on as soon as I saw you."

Blinders. Riley has a pair, somewhere, but she never remembers them when she leaves the house, because why would she require them? Dark glasses made from welder's glass, the kind of thing someone might wear to glimpse an eclipse at the moment of totality. Impractical for routine prophylactic wear, because you can't see a damn thing. They're split-second shields, used at the instant of need.

They should both be safe now. But Riley won't raise her eyes any farther than she's already done. Because *should be* is not *is*.

People have died screaming because of *should be*.

"I'm new in the neighborhood." Soft, musical laugh. "Whatever *neighborhood* means, I guess. Nobody's out here, right? I live about a mile up the road."

Riley imagines a gesture. A hand indicating direction.

"Been here a few weeks now," the voice continues. "Finally wanted to venture out a bit. I honestly didn't think anyone was around. Most I've seen was a mail drone."

"No one is around," Riley croaks. Her own voice is bizarrely rough in her ears. This shouldn't be happening. Whoever this is should not be here. Why are they here? Why are they *talking* to her? Why the fuck take that risk?

"Which is why I moved here. Why I guess anyone moves here. But I saw you, I figured I'd come say hello."

"Why?"

A tone has the capacity to convey a shrug. "Not sure. I know maybe I shouldn't, I—" Unease now. "I can go, I'm sorry."

"No." Riley stops, stunned by herself. *Going* is exactly what this person should be doing, and as soon as possible. They could both die, hideously. Easily.

And yet.

"It's all right," she says—an echo. "I haven't seen anyone in . . ." She can't think. Time is no solid thing but a collection of tiny loose particles, disorganized moments slipping like sand through her fingers. "A long time."

"Yeah, me neither. Was holed up in this ugly little gated community about thirty miles from here, but my parents had a vacation place and I finally figured I might as well head there. Here. Get some freedom." Pause. "Actually be able to go outside and walk around. You know? The community association never allowed that, not unless you had official dispensation. Even though hardly anyone was left. Probably I should have gotten used to that, it's been years, but I never could." Another pause. "I'm talking too much, aren't I?"

"No, I . . ." *I don't know what counts as too much.* "I just don't have a lot to say."

What's to lose in honesty?

"How long have you been here?"

Riley frowns. "I'm not sure."

"Yeah, time is weird now, isn't it?" Movement in the upper-left periphery of Riley's vision and the sound of scuffling: the boots moving on cracked asphalt, the shifting dapple of the sunlight. "It's not just being inside all the time either. It's more than that." Another laugh, now wry. "Fucking listen to me, I met you like five minutes ago and I'm getting all deep."

Riley nods and doesn't laugh. Nothing about this strikes her as unreasonable, except for the fact that it's happening at all. "It's weird talking to people. It's like it's not the same . . ."

"It's not the same pattern anymore."

"Yes," Riley says, a little surprised by how well that fits. "That's exactly how it is."

She's discovering this second by second. It's completely different when it's text.

"People used to start with names, didn't they?" Hint of a smile in the stretch of the vowels. "What's your name?"

"Riley."

"Hello, Riley. I'm Ellis."

"Hello, Ellis."

It's not the same pattern anymore. But she's remembering the tiniest bit of what that pattern was like, and when her own smile finds her lips, it's strained.

6

She thinks, albeit with less and less frequency, about the first time she left the apartment after it all started.

How long into the whole thing? *The pandemic*, some people were calling it by then, but Riley never felt like that fit; can you have a pandemic with no identifiable cause, no squirming little organism to be isolated under a microscope? In any case, it couldn't have been more than two weeks. She was afraid to leave, but at that point, fear itself was beginning to be so much more like weariness than anything else, no more restraining than being tired after a long fucking week.

Sometimes what you really want, when you're tired like that, is a walk.

So she took one. Put on a pair of the darkest sunglasses she owned—in the midst of sporadic lockdowns, people were experimenting with those as a form of protective gear, with unfortunately mixed success—and eased her way down the two flights of stairs, opened and closed the front door like a teenager sneaking out for a party. Like she was worried someone would see her and—what? Call the cops or something? No official stay-at-home order was being enforced, not right then, and cops were responding to calls with even less reliability than usual anyway. Get aggressively judgmental about her irresponsibility? Yell at her? Call her names?

Kill her with their bare hands?

There was no one out there anyway. She blinked at the street through the darkened lenses; it was not a sunny day, and everything appeared flat and colorless in a way the glasses couldn't account for. Deserted street, more silent than in any dead of night, with neat rows of cars lining either side.

Everyone else was huddled inside, too.

Traffic noise, but distant—at least it was some indication that this surreal dream of silent absence didn't extend everywhere. She was still groping for normality then, an impulse she now regards with vague scorn because it was so utterly useless. She would have done better to settle for the facts, adapt to them and figure out what came next. Instead, she was stubbornly looking backward through her insufficiently dark glasses and hoping that things might somehow go back to the way they were.

Naive idiocy. Christ, she was lucky to survive long enough to realize what it was.

She made her way slowly down the middle of the street, listening. For voices, for the sound of a TV, a stereo, for a closer car, for the gentle whirring click of a bike's wheels, for literally anything. There was nothing. Yet there was no real sense of absence. There were people behind those shut doors and drawn curtains and closed blinds. She could feel them, could practically smell them; the odor of their fear tinted the air yellowish and sour like a ruptured sewer pipe. She regarded that fear with nothing but bewildered respect; what she was acting on wasn't bravery, and she had no illusions there. If she was smart, if she had sense, if she had a properly functioning instinct for self-preservation and any consideration for the safety of others, she would have been staying the fuck inside.

But in strange times, we do strange things. And sometimes our selves aren't so interested in preservation.

She walked a block, another one, found herself moving in a circle. Twice, she caught the twitch of blinds, the snatch of a face there and then gone. Once on the sidewalk, a man hurrying by—she thought it was probably a man but she wasn't certain—with his head down and turned away. She turned away as well. As she did so, she was aware that her eyes were burning.

She didn't know what any of it meant. She was and is pretty sure that no one did. How do you comprehend something like this? How do you watch a shaky cell phone video of three construction workers killing one another with hammers and incorporate that into any kind of sense-making?

She ducked into an alley and braced her back against the wall, pulled off her glasses, and pressed her face into her sweaty palms until she managed to go home. Memory is unreliable, especially now, but she thinks she didn't leave her apartment again for well over a week.

In the end, maybe it's disturbing how easy it was to adjust. How easy it is for the worst things imaginable to become normal.

Or maybe, she's wondered more than once, that was just her finding it so easy. If so, she's wondered about what that would mean.

7

At home, putting away the groceries. Falling light easing across the threadbare rug in the living room. Riley half expected Ellis to offer to help carry the boxes. But Ellis didn't. Ellis left not long after the ritual exchange of names, and with the slightest air of awkwardness. As if goodbye is a difficult thing to find one's way to.

Riley feels like maybe that was always true.

But she barely remembers, so who the fuck knows.

She has to incorporate this somehow, she thinks as she stacks cans in the cramped pantry—she already has enough food to get through a good three or four months of total isolation. This new thing, this new element of life. There is a person here. Not very close but not very far—within walking distance. She knows the destination because she heard Ellis returning that way. How easy it would be to go there now. Go there anytime. Ellis said nothing about it, but Riley somehow intuits that if she did show up there, uninvited and unannounced, Ellis wouldn't chase her off. Which is what any reasonable person should do, but no reasonable person would have said hello to her in the first place, so *here the fuck we are*.

She puts away the rest of the cans, the boxes. Goes to

the small living room and sinks into the ratty old recliner in the corner, gazes at the falling light through the wide bay window opposite. Looks down at her bare feet and thinks about shoes. Thinks about that ankle, the hint of gray sock. The shoes not her own, on feet not hers. Another of the early days, when she once more found herself at her apartment window, and in the street by her front stoop lay two feet attached to legs attached to nothing at all. Flesh sheared off beneath the pelvis but the severed pieces bizarrely aligned, as if attached to a body unseen. How the separation happened so neatly was mysterious, but the separation itself was not: a city bus rammed headlong into an ambulance, both at full speed. As if aiming for each other.

Because they were. Of course they were.

Riley wiggles her toes. For a split second, she wonders what she would have done if they had remained still.

She's gotten so weird, and there's another person, and for some reason, they seemed interested in her, and they aren't far away, and she could go see them now if she wanted to.

Except no. Seeing is precisely what she can't do.

8

Groping through a world without eyes.

A blurry gray mass of indistinct people behind thick lenses, a world gone apocalyptic with artificial darkness. Not dreamlike at all but horrifyingly banal in its sheer reality. The swiftness of adjustment, accommodation. You get used to the unthinkable so unbelievably quickly. A fragmentary yet intensely vivid memory: a low-lit college lecture hall, and on the lowered screen at the front, starving Ukrainian peasants gazing at her with their hollow, haunted eyes.

They ate one another, she heard. They ate their friends and neighbors, their children, their siblings and parents, now and then themselves. First it was horrifying. Then it was merely shameful. Then it was routine.

You adjust. You accommodate.

Or you seize the alternatives. The suicide rate soaring in the weeks and months after the outbreak, not suicides of madness but instead calculated choices, sometimes with explanatory notes and sometimes without. Alone. Always alone. The truth is that the best-case scenario was dying alone, because dying in the company of others was nearly without exception infinitely worse.

Their deaths belong to them, Riley thought. She had begun to turn away from the news and the net by then. None of it was actually new anymore. Doctors and scientists remained bewildered. Public health recommendations had not progressed beyond staying inside and avoiding looking at anyone's face. It seemed there was nothing else to learn.

But: *their deaths belong to them.* They own the means, the manner, the timing of it. They own what people take from it, sense or nonsense. Isn't that better than the alternative?

Isn't that almost admirable?

She never once considered suicide, is the odd thing. She never once considered seizing that power for herself. She dropped her eyes, closed them, covered them, wandered through a city that was beginning to empty out as everyone fled everyone else. During the Black Death, people fled to the countrysides. Other people were a potentially diseased and death-dealing terror. They hid in the shadows of forests and fields. Sometimes they told stories.

What stories will we tell about this? If anyone survives, what legends will they concoct about this time? When they look back at us, what will they see?

If they can look. If they can see. If the plague ended. If everything has changed.

9

In the moonlight, Riley walks.

The gravel drive is a gray-silver dream pathway snaking ahead of her, the trees leaning over it to form an angular arch beneath which she passes. Night birds flit and call above her. The snatches of bruise-tinted sky are starless, washed out in the light of that moon. It's nearly full. Is it waxing or waning? Riley had an astronomy app on her phone that could have told her. Only now does she fully understand that the phone was one of her last remaining tethers to linear time, and with it buried in the mud at the bottom of the lake, she has no anchor.

Floating down the drive toward the road.

The birds softly call and the trees whisper in the breeze, but around her is a pocket of silence. Not even the creak of the gravel under her shoes. Not even her own breath. It occurs to her that she might be dreaming—and isn't this very much adhering to the logic of a dream? Some unarticulated impulse tugging her toward something she doesn't fully understand.

A whisper of dread low in her belly, like a cluster of uneasy trees in her core.

But only a whisper, and only low. She's as calm as the moonlight. She reaches the gate and opens it without consciously choosing to do so; she opens it because she does, and according to the same reasoning, she steps out onto the road, moves to its center, and stands motionless, fully exposed to the sky. An eye in negative. The moon a pupil virtually too bright to look directly at, nestled in the middle of blue-black sclera.

She does tip her head back and look directly at it. Unblinking. An edge of ludicrous defiance. *Come at me.*

I'm already out of my fucking mind.

You can't win a staring contest with the sky. Eventually, she lowers her eyes, sucks in a breath. Turns in place, glances up and down the road. The gravel was silver; the road is a river of blackness, ominous and strange.

She isn't altogether certain anymore that she knows which way to go. She can't remember. She can't remember how she thought she knew.

But she also feels that she doesn't need to know. Because this is either a dream or the logic of a dream, and in the end, she doubts the distinction matters much.

She closes her eyes and turns, turns again. Stops, eyes still closed, and begins to walk.

She left the silence behind at the gate. She hears herself now: the scuffle of her feet, the faint whoosh of her breathing. The click of an ankle once injured playing soccer and never properly healed. The world is still dreamlike, but with every step, it's also increasingly vivid. The shadows are hardening, the light a glare. She's beginning to feel uncomfortably exposed, like a rodent with no cover from the claws of a descending hawk.

She doesn't turn around.

She passes other gates almost identical to hers, rusting mailboxes long deprived of mail. Other drives, with empty houses at the end of them. That absence has always been reassuring to her; now it's unsettling. Would it be better to know someone's there, even if she never speaks to them?

The road curves. She feels a centrifugal pull as she follows. She glances to the left, the outer edge of the arc, and there's the gate; somehow she knows that it's the one she's been heading for this entire time, and she halts and turns and stares at it.

As with the others, it's very like her own.

Is it locked? She sees only a simple latch. Her hands open and close; she can feel the cool metal against her palms, so intense and real that she expects to look down and see that she's touching the top bar and preparing to push it open.

It seems strange to her that it isn't locked, although it would be a simple matter to hop over. It's barely a barrier at all.

Ellis struck her as remarkably, almost unbelievably unafraid.

But that's the thing. What is there to fear now? Not that someone will come for you, not if they aren't infected. People stay away. And the infected scarcely survive long enough to do much of anything to anyone who isn't in immediate proximity to them.

When they can't kill anyone else, there's always themselves.

She isn't touching the gate. She can't see the house from the road—again, like her own. Not even a flicker of light through the trees.

What would happen, if she opened the gate and walked up the drive and knocked on the door?

She has no blindfold, no glasses, no blinders. Only her naked eyes. She feels, ridiculously, that it would be not only fantastically dangerous but also scandalous, like showing up literally naked. But what would happen?

Is Ellis even there? Was any of that real?

If you lost your mind, how would you know?

Do the infected know they've gone insane, even as they're murdering whatever they can reach?

Go home. Go home now. Stop this.

After a while, she turns around and makes her way slowly back down the road to her own gate, her own drive, her own house. The safe little corner of the world she's made for herself, and as with herself and time, she now understands that it's coming untethered, that she's been subconsciously but systematically cutting the last bonds between it and everything else.

And it comes to her to wonder why. But by then, she's falling asleep in the recliner, and the moon has set, and she's drifting again.

10

In the brilliance of late-morning sunlight, she finds herself at the gate again, and this time, there's no mistaking it for any kind of dream.

Unless life is *but a blah blah blah*.

Like the night before, she stands and stares, her fingers twitching at her sides. In one hand are her blinders; unfolded and ready to slide on, but she hasn't, and it hits her that Ellis could come sauntering around the drive's bend at any time, emerge from the trees with an uncovered face and unguarded eyes.

Does Ellis *saunter*? she wonders.

In any case. She chews her bottom lip, glances down at the blinders. Black bulbous lenses gleam in the sun. A fragment of her own reflection: warped and stretched like a funhouse mirror, her bare outlines with scarcely a visible feature. Faceless.

Safe.

Turn around. Turn around and go the hell home. This is crazy. What are you doing it for anyway? Why would you ever risk it? Impose the risk on both of you? For what? What are you getting out of this? Why are you here at all?

She literally can't recall the last time she went somewhere with the express purpose of human interaction.

Her hands are on the gate, running over the warm metal, curling around it without pushing or pulling. She feels its solidity and also how it would move quite easily, the promise of smoothness in the hinges. Freshly oiled, maybe. She thinks of her own place, where it's been forever since she applied oil to much of anything except food.

The latch is indeed not locked in any way that would require a code or key. Riley unlatches it and takes satisfaction in the expected smoothness of its inward swing.

It's not as if she's committed beyond return at this point. She could turn around anytime. She has a bit of driveway before she reaches the house. There's still time for changing one's mind.

She latches the gate behind her and starts to walk.

One foot proverbially in front of the other. Her hands swing at her sides. It comes to her that perhaps she should have brought something baked or a casserole of some kind, a recognition of the old customs of neighborhood welcome. Observing them would have been patently absurd, but then again, so is all of this, so why the fuck not?

Laughter bubbles up in her throat, and it feels faintly hysterical, like if she let it out it might scare the birds. The sound bursting out of her, many pairs of wings exploding from the treetops. She isn't turning around. Every second she doesn't is a second in which she makes the choice to keep going, actively and consciously; chiseling away at any remaining excuses.

So if Ellis demands to know what she's doing here, what will she say?

What were you doing at my gate yesterday?

An argument could be made for them both being equally culpable.

The drive ends rather abruptly, widens and branches on the left to a garage, on the right up to a low set of porch steps and the front door beyond.

Riley halts as abruptly as the drive does, and stares at the house.

Same size as hers. Same basic architecture, surrounded in a wide rough circle by tall beeches and pines. But, as if the gate was an indication of overall state: as neat as hers isn't, as well kept as hers hasn't been in multiple years. The pale yellow paint on the siding looks relatively fresh. The roof is missing some tiles, but the mix of dull mossy ones and clean ones suggests that they are—or recently were—in the process of being replaced. Her gaze lands on the ladder just visible around the side; confirmation. Ellis is fixing the place up.

Why?

Well, why not?

All at once, Riley feels awkward, uncertain about what to do next. Call out? Walk boldly up the porch steps and rap her knuckles against the screen door? Is there a bell? Should she ring it? What's the etiquette for this situation? What was it ever?

As it turns out, Ellis saves her from having to figure it out on her own by swinging the door open and emerging into the shade of the porch.

Not enough shade to conceal anything much. Every muscle in Riley's body goes rigid with instinctive fear. The flash of a face in gentle shadow, a shard of it like a hazy reflection in a broken mirror. She flings her gaze away: the Virginia creeper snaking its way up the nearest tree, half starburst of leaves nodding in the breeze. She will not think about the face. As quickly as she processes that she saw it at all, her memory is wiping all trace of it, as if the memory itself could attack her brain.

There's no evidence that such a thing is possible, but evidence only counts for so much.

And what the hell is even going on out there, in the world beyond the cabins and the lake and the trees? Does she even really know?

If some new and dangerous development presented itself, she probably wouldn't know about it. Not until it was too late.

"Riley?" Ellis sounds surprised—only slightly. Not unpleasantly. No anger detectable at nearly being forced into a potentially lethal encounter. "Holy shit, what are you—" *Doing here,* is the obvious end to that query, but Ellis cuts it off and huffs a laugh. "Guess I'd have suggested you give me a heads-up before you came over, but I never gave you my number."

"I don't have a phone." Riley is playing with the blinders again, as if she isn't certain what to do with them—which is idiocy. Don't they exist for one purpose only? She pulls in a breath and slides them on, although she keeps her gaze firmly averted. "Sorry."

"You don't?"

"No." Pause. She's finding that she has no idea how much to share, how much would be *over*sharing, what level of frankness is appropriate here. "I threw it in the lake."

"Did you now." Ellis sounds bemused. "Why would you go and do a thing like that?"

"No real reason." *I don't really know* doesn't seem like an adequate response, although it would be the most honest one available to her.

"No landline?"

"No," she replies. Not a functioning one, not so far as she knows. She's never paid the bill.

"Well." Tone indicating that Ellis is prepared to move on from the subject of phones unless Riley would like it to continue. "Good to know, I guess. Good to see you, too." See you. For some reason, that strikes Riley as funny. "Do you want to come in?"

Come in.

The question hangs in the air between them, like something Ellis has extended toward her on a pole. Not bait on a fishing line. Nothing so sinister. But it's being held out to her, and unless she does something with it, it'll continue to hang there, getting more and more awkward in a more and more pronounced fashion.

Do you want to come in.

She can't get her hands around it. So can't take it. Can't do anything with it. She has been invited inside someone else's house. Someone else's bubble of safety—because your living space, if you live alone, which by now almost everyone must—is the only space over which you have anything approaching total control. Another human being with eyes and a brain is a wild card, treacherous and unpredictable, fully able to murder both intentionally or by accident. Or be murdered. Taking Ellis's proffered hand is stepping into a minefield.

Dancing.

Riley shakes herself. She needs to answer. Something. Or spin on her heel and tear-ass two-thirds blind down the drive to the road.

She swallows hard enough to make her throat click in her ears, and goes rigid and muscle-scared once more when she hears herself agreeing.

11

She should clearly remember the last time she saw her mother face-to-face. She doesn't. Only retains flashes, fragments—like a broken mirror. Perhaps it comes to her in that way because what she retains of the final—the final two or three—encounters with her one surviving parent and last surviving family is so marked by the sharp glitter of shattered glass scattered across the floor.

Standing in the foyer of her mother's small bungalow. Suburbs, night, silent with few lights visible. Out of rage or despair or pure pragmatic mistrust of illumination, some-one knocked out all the streetlights. Inside her mother's house, the only light is from the waning half-moon. It catches the glass on the foyer's floor, the hardwood and the old mud rug, and the glass seems to intensify and magnify it. It strikes her eyes like tiny needles, and she looks away.

Not the last time she saw her. The glass was broken before then, surely. Everyone was trashing their mirrors. It was practically a joke. All that bad luck accumulating, hanging over cities like toxic smog, blanketing the future and foreclosing on recovery. However such recovery might have come. *At this rate, we'll never get out of it.*

Her mother's voice from the gloom. Low, quavery in a way Riley doesn't like. Her mother was always firm, usually confident, sometimes aggressive. Her voice was robust and a little husky from an earlier life of cigarette consumption. Nothing like how she sounds now. *Riley? Honey? Is that you?*

Of course it was Riley. She was the only other person, so far as she knew, who had a key.

Stepping gingerly over the glass. She doesn't manage to avoid it entirely, and it grits beneath her heel. *You should clean this stuff up, Mom. You could hurt yourself.*

If I try to clean it up, I could hurt myself, too, comes the voice—weak, faint, and somehow echoing as if from the depths of a cave. *It's mostly just by the door. I don't go near the door anymore.*

Not at all? How does she eat? What if something happens? What if she needs a doctor? Doctors are still a thing, along with a great deal else of the world Before; even now, so much of that world slogs stubbornly and grimly and absurdly onward. Later she will come to think of it as a zombie, a rotting thing shambling along with its intestines dangling from its belly in slimy ropes, too mindless to understand that it should lie down and be dead.

It's stunned her, how many things don't change much when so many other things do.

But Mom doesn't go near the door anymore.

Something is wrong, something beyond the obvious.

Mom. Her voice sounds very small and very young in the darkness. Through the foyer and into the front hall; peering into the living and dining rooms, Riley sees that

Mom is not satisfied with the dark of the night; she's pulled blackout curtains over all the windows. *Mom, where are you?*

And Mom calls softly that she's in the bedroom.

If this wasn't the last time Riley saw her, what happened in the times after this one? What was the aftermath? In the months and years after she finds herself groping for any clarity where that's concerned, even as she shies away from the memory. She's seen so many horrible things by now, she believes herself numb, her emotional landscape eroded into slatey flatness by ceaseless storms. One more horror should make no difference.

She picks her way down the hall toward the rear of the house. The bedroom, which her mother and father occupied since they sold the old house after Riley went to college, and which her mother has occupied since her father died nearly ten years ago. Riley has never really felt at home in this house—there's no reason why she should—but it never felt outright hostile.

Now it's as if hundreds of eyes are staring at her through the membrane of the unseen walls.

She keeps her own eyes fixed on the blackness in front of her. Clutched in one hand, damp with her sweaty palm, is a blindfold; she doesn't remember retrieving it from her pocket. She won't be able to look at her mother's face. She still hasn't fully come to terms with that, that on a deep level she'll never really see her mother's face again.

The bedroom door is ajar on the left. She pauses at it, presses her fingertips lightly against its slightly grainy surface. Something about the quality of the paint. She closes her eyes and takes the texture in, the solidity, and listens for any sounds of life behind it.

Riley? Honey? A pause. Heavy breathing. *You can come in, sweetheart. You don't need to bother with covering up.*

Why wouldn't she? Why the hell? Why is her mother inviting her to take on a deadly level of risk? Maybe Mom has simply taken leave of her senses, sunk into a swamp of denial; she wouldn't be the first one.

It's okay, sweetheart. I promise. It's all safe now.

Which is when she knows what's happened. So she pushes open the door, pulls out her cell phone, and—hands shaking now as well as sweating—she turns on the flashlight function.

Madness. But the whole room stinks of madness. She smells it the second she sets a foot across the threshold. She's learned that it's not a false cliché; insanity does indeed have its own scent. Pheromones, maybe, or something along those lines. The smell is sickly and acrid, between cleaning chemicals and vinegar. Not intense but unmistakable.

Floor littered with unfolded clothes, food containers, assorted trash. Mom was very neat, once. Riley tracks the light across the floor to the bed and raises it, guides it across the rumpled bedspread to a pair of bent legs clad in red flannel pajamas. Matching top. Her mother looks so tiny, leaning back against a mountain of pillows. Her right hand lies loose by her hip. She's holding something that glitters silver and crimson and sharp.

Riley hauls in an enormous, trembling breath and the light meets her mother's face, and her mother's eyes are gone.

Riley holds the light and gazes blankly at her. Her mother offers her a weak smile.

You see? No more problem.

Yes. No more problem.

People have been taking this approach. There are helpful step-by-step instructions online, how to do it with minimum mess and pain and risk of infection. Mom must not have consulted those instructions. None of them would ever have counseled her to do it like this.

Riley licks her lips and tastes nothing. She's not rushing to the bed, screaming, tearing into the pillows, clawing at the sheets, pulling her mother into her arms and bursting into hysterical tears. She's just dimly annoyed at her mother for blinding herself by a careless and imprudent method.

She lowers the light and goes to the bathroom to wet a towel and find some antibiotic ointment. She will not call the hospital or the doctor, although she knows she should.

Maybe this is the last time she sees her mother. Maybe it's the second or third to last. It doesn't matter, because it makes no difference to the end. Her mother will wander into the street—Christ only knows why—and be run down by an old Ford pickup, in the cab of which are a middle-aged brother and sister trying like hell to murder each other. Riley's mother will die under the wheels, her spine crushed. The woman will succeed in strangling her brother; she will then beat her own skull in against the pavement. There won't be a funeral. Funerals are a rarity, although they do happen.

Last times are last times. Maybe it doesn't matter whether you remember when specifically they happened.

What matters is that everything stopped then, and nothing came after.

Only they did. That's the truly crazy thing. Somehow they did.

Somehow it all just keeps on going.

12

"You can take the blinders off. I'm going into the kitchen to make tea." Ellis's voice coming from the moving shadow directly ahead of Riley. "There's no direct line of sight. I'll yell before I come back in."

Ellis doesn't wait for Riley's murmured assent. It takes Riley a few seconds, the blinders wobbling slightly between her fingertips, to realize that Ellis also didn't ask whether Riley wanted tea in the first place. She does. Tea sounds wonderful.

Footsteps behind her, fading toward the back of the house.

Blinking, Riley looks around.

The similarities between her place and this one apparently end at the outside. Where Riley's place is cluttered and dusty and old, all the décor decades out of date and all the fabric threadbare, Ellis's is very neat and very spare, and also quite bright, with all the blinds pulled up and the color scheme comprised of blues and yellows offset by a few darker jewel tones. The furniture is IKEA-chic without looking cheap. The shelves are mostly covered with books, but here and there are other items, all of them oddly devoid of clearly recognizable form. Abstract crystal and polished stone that almost look like something real. Pots and vases decorated with complex designs all swoops and curving weaves like the patterns in a mosque.

The one thing in abundance, aside from the books, is the art on the walls.

Slowly, Riley turns and scans the room in a circuit. A good two-thirds of the available space is occupied. None of them are paintings as far as she can see; it's all photography, much of it in black and white or sepia but some in vibrant color. Landscapes—forests, mountains, frozen fields, an expanse of tawny desert under an aggressively blue sky. Structures—old churches, skyscrapers, windmills, abandoned and half-collapsed barns. Animals—birds. A white cloud of snow geese captured in mid-eruption from a pond soaked in golden evening. Pigeons on a wire. The keen, skeptical eye of a crow. This last Riley spends some time on. An eye, which can be viewed in safety.

"Coming in."

Riley jumps. Glances around. She's standing in front of the photo of the crow, close. She doesn't know when she moved. She fumbles with the blinders, gets them on, turns and faces the world in blurry shadows in shades of dark gray and black. She can see well enough to negotiate her way to one of the armchairs arranged around the glossy wood coffee table, she thinks.

Ellis is by the other chair. Bending. Putting the mugs down. Does Ellis have anything on? Riley suddenly finds herself wondering and dislikes it; it feels far too much like suspicion.

She's freshly cognizant of how vulnerable she is, with someone else here in this space that is not her own. But she would be almost as vulnerable in her own space.

It's people who are the danger.

Warm ceramic nudges her hands. She takes the mug reflexively, lifts it, and inhales the heavy scent of black tea accented with something floral.

Rose.

"Is that okay?"

"It's fine." Riley takes a cautious sip.

"I should have asked if you liked it sweetened. I almost never do. I feel like it gets in the way of, y'know, the aromatic part."

"It's fine," Riley murmurs again and then feels that she should say something more. "I usually don't sweeten it either."

Which isn't all that true. She wonders why she lied. It seems a weird and faintly troubling thing to do as a default, more troubling to do it and not know why.

"I was looking at the photos," she goes on, eager to slide the subject to something less problematic than tea preferences. "I like them. They're very . . . diverse."

"Oh. Thank you." Ellis sounds pleased and a little surprised. "I took them."

"Really? All of them?" Which clangs as a stupid question in her own ear. She is remarkably bad at this, at conversation, but as soon as the thought comes to her, she's in doubt about how good she was at it to begin with. Whether it was always hard and awkward and shitty.

"Mm-hmm." Nothing detectable in Ellis's tone regarding the stupidity of the question anyway. "Been a photographer most of my life. Just amateur, I never took any classes or anything."

"Oh." Riley sips her tea. The chair is very comfortable. She resists the urge to sit back and let herself sink into the cushions. "I wouldn't have been able to tell. They're very good. Or I mean . . . I think they are, I don't know, I don't know anything about art."

Talking fast. Too fast? Is it bad form to negate one's own compliment like that? Is that in fact what she did?

"I think they are, too," Ellis says quietly. "I think it's ridiculous to pretend you don't think you're talented at something, when you know you are. I loved it. For itself, that is. I never thought about trying to sell them or exhibit them or anything. I used to give them to friends as gifts."

"What do you like photographing best?" It is polite, Riley thinks, to express interest in someone else's interest and ask them a question about it.

But also she discovers that she wants to know.

"People," Ellis says, even quieter. "I used to do a lot of portraits. That's what most of the gifts were."

Riley is silent. She feels as if she's come to the end of a series of walkways set over a network of long, snaking gorges, rushing water far below, and now she stands on the broken edge, the rest of the thing sheared off by a storm or a hard wind. She didn't expect it and she's teetering just a bit.

There are no people in any of the photographs she saw.

Not merely no faces. No people.

"You must have seen there aren't any in any of the ones I've got on the walls." Still quiet. Thinly amused.

There's a bitterness in that amusement that strikes in Riley's core and resonates like a distant bell. She marvels at it. "I packed them all away in the early days, when we didn't know whether someone needed to be . . . real and alive and there for it to happen, or whether even a picture would be enough. And I just never unpacked them after that."

"Makes sense," Riley murmurs. "We still haven't really cleared that part up for sure one way or the other." She pauses a beat. "Unless something changed that I don't know about."

The click of Ellis's throat. A swallow. "You're not too plugged into the outside, are you? Of course you aren't, you threw away your phone."

"I stopped checking the news a long time ago."

"Me, too." Ellis exhales. "Didn't seem to be a point anymore."

"But you still have them? The portraits?"

"Yeah, somewhere." But Ellis's tone is markedly vague. Evasive? Perhaps. "It's hard to get rid of your own work. Even if it might be a good idea." Another swallow, another exhalation, and the creak of shifting weight in the chair. The sway and shift of the shadows. "What about you? What do you do?"

Riley stares down at the mug in her hands—in the direction of it. She moves her fingers across its smooth curve, searching absently for the minute telltale ridges that might indicate a pattern. She can't tell what color it is. It merely looks dark.

Could peek.

She shoves the thought away and shrugs. "I don't know."

Ellis barks a laugh. "How can you not know what you do?"

"I don't know," Riley repeats, something coiling defensively in her middle. The question abruptly feels intrusive, unwelcome, as if she's being asked to justify her persistent existence. "I do . . . whatever. I go for walks, I read."

"What do you read?"

"Whatever's lying around." She's unable to keep the exasperation out of her voice—and unable to conceal from herself the truth behind the exasperation, which is that she's unsettled all over again, hopelessly wrong-footed by a stranger in a strange space.

Afraid. A little.

"I'm not interrogating you," Ellis says, quiet again. "I'm just curious. I'm interested in you. You don't have to tell me anything you don't want to."

Riley is silent. The silence is a retreat. Yet it feels no more secure than the words did. She grips the mug so tightly that her hands tremble, her knees pressed together and her back rigid. She's uncomfortably aware of these things, the position of her muscles and the attitude of her frame, and of the shallow twitch of her lungs. She's afraid, and she's embarrassed about being afraid, and she's angry about being embarrassed, and the anger is pitiful and aimless. She follows the thread of her emotions, the jump from one to the other, with a familiar detachment that nevertheless makes nothing any easier.

"It's like we said," she whispers as the words return to her. "It's weird talking to people. It's weird because I haven't done it in a really long time."

"It's weird talking to people because it can get you killed," Ellis says simply.

Riley jerks her head up. The movement jars the blinders, and her lungs cease their twitching as the left blinder arm slips from behind her ear. The light slams into her eye, ruthless and ten times as brilliant as it was when she'd walked in, and a little cry breaks out of her, followed by the bizarrely tuneful sound of the mug shattering on the hardwood as she grabs convulsively at the blinder frames.

The darkness returns.

She makes sure they're secure, bends and fumbles for the shards of ceramic. Cursing. Cursing again at the sparkle of pain when one of them slices the pad of her thumb. The blinders aren't the goggles that many people came to favor, but they do come with an elastic band to fix around the back of the head. She didn't use it. Why didn't she use it? Why the fuck didn't she use it? What was she thinking, coming here and not using it?

"I'm sorry," she mutters. "Shit, I'm sorry, I'm—"

"It's okay." The air is displaced, and against her exposed arm she feels the radiated heat and solid presence of another body near to hers. "You don't have to worry about it, I'll get it after—"

Warm roughness brushes the side of her hand, and she yanks it away with a hiss of breath. Freezes. Ellis has frozen as well.

The point of contact is tingling slightly, as though someone has poured weak acid on it.

Later, lying in bed and wholly unable to sleep, Riley will trace her fingers over that spot and feel the tingle again, and she'll recall reading once that physical contact is, in a way, a tactile illusion. That atoms can never really touch, that particles always repel one another.

She has never truly been touched, and she never will be.

Riley straightens. It's a sharp, stiff movement. "I should go. I'm sorry," she says again, and she means it with a ferocity that she doesn't at all understand.

A rising shadow. Ellis standing as well. "I'm sorry, too."

Tone unreadable now.

"It's not you." There's a desperate edge in the words. "It's—like I said, I'm just—I'm not used to it. It's not you."

"I know." Ellis moving away. "I'm going back to the kitchen. You can take off the blinders in a couple of seconds. Seriously, don't worry about the mug."

Riley nods, and as gestures go, it feels stupid and useless. She waits until she hears Ellis stop moving, hears the call of all right. She slides the blinders off and, blinking hard, stumbles to the door. The sun is bright and without mercy, and she shields her eyes with her upraised hand as she hurries down the porch steps. Squeak-clack of the screen door, creak of the boards under her shoes. Then the gravel, and she's nearly running down the drive, into the dimmer relief of the tree cover.

She wonders, if she turned now, what she would see. A face at the door, at the window, watching her.

She doesn't turn. And perhaps the hot pressure on the back of her neck is only her imagination.

That's what she'll choose to believe.

13

Dull impatience, back then, over what *contact* and *interaction* meant.

More specifically over how they were used and the ways in which that use was contested. Think pieces and Twitter threads and punditry professional and amateur, and all as obnoxious as such things usually are. What will it do to people to no longer interact the way they always have? What will it mean when so many have so little contact with one another? Well, what does any of that have to do with anything? How do people make contact? How do they interact? You don't need sight to do any of that. It's not as though blind people live in a sensory hermitage, Riley thought.

And of course it wasn't long before blind people were fetishized in a whole new and uniformly gross way; Riley wasn't disabled, not to speak of, but she could only imagine what it must be like to experience such sudden and surreal and unwanted . . .

Well, visibility.

But what did contact mean? Interaction? Isolation? What was it, to see eyes? To see a face? To no longer see? Certainly not the end of the world. And the world wasn't ending; it was stubbornly chugging along, albeit not very well.

At some point, wasn't it ridiculous anyway how academic the conversation got? Like a discursive defense mechanism. What you're talking about is the fact that you can't look at someone's face without risking bloody, shrieking death. What you're talking about is literally visceral. Literal blood and literal guts. Raw empty eye sockets. In the face of such things, words melt away. Not everyone sees, not everyone likes making eye contact, and this picture is always more complicated than the discourse reflects, but the empty eye sockets are what Riley always comes back to in the end, because it's the emptiness, because it's the confusion of the emptiness, and it's also the fact that it isn't so much emptiness as all the furniture constantly rearranged in a pitch-black room.

Stumbling around and groping at something and at nothing. We can't learn from this, one thinks. We always adapt, but that doesn't always mean we learn.

It doesn't always mean we survive.

If it comes right down to it, what is survival supposed to mean? What does that look like now?

That pitch-black room. Standing in its midst, the sound of your blinking eyelids like the click of insects. The rush of your breathing. Too afraid to take a step.

It looks like nothing at all. That's the point.

14

Riley sits in the recliner with her fingertips pressed against her eyes until white-gold fireworks burst in an internal night sky the color of oxygen-starved blood.

She's thinking of when she burned every image of a human face. She had already smashed all the mirrors and thrown out every sufficiently reflective surface. It was, admittedly, a little hysterical.

Only was it?

The week after she came to live here. Worked up the energy and then worked up the courage to scour the place, tear it apart, haul out boxes of books, and rip pictures from frames. There's an old firepit behind the house, and in it, she piled all those faces and doused them with lighter fluid and tossed a match. The smell of the smoke was not pleasing. She stood there, wrapped in a shawl against the chilly wind coming off the lake, and she considered funeral pyres.

All the bodies are burned now.

She closed her eyes and fantasized about stray sparks igniting dry leaves and twigs, licking up the tree trunks and gilding the branches with dancing flames. Sweeping over the house, crawling along the drive toward the road. Eating the forest all the way down to the water's edge. In this fantasy, she placed herself in the water, floating naked on her back and watching the world burn.

Once the faces had bubbled and melted, she made herself look at them. It might have been the acrid smoke making her eyes sting.

She drops her hands and gets unsteadily to her feet. Hardly any lights are on, but yet again, everything is too bright.

I'm lost, she hears herself whisper, and she doesn't know what it means.

Riley wanders aimlessly through the house. It's past midnight and the place feels cavernous, bigger inside than the exterior would suggest. She *could* get lost in here. When she was very small and came out here for summer visits, the whole place felt enormous in comparison to their cramped little apartment in the city. It should probably have been fun, but she always found it a little frightening, and the forest seemed to press against the windows, many shadowy figures with unseen eyes crowded against the glass. Fogging it with their breath.

Fogging it with their breath.

She freezes, staring at the windowpane. She didn't draw this curtain when the sun went down. It reflects, although only barely, only in shadows and outlines like a blinder of its own, she can't see her own face at all. She sees her unkempt shoulder-length hair, her rigid shoulders, her skinny frame.

Dimly realizes that she hasn't really seen herself in years.

But that's all beside the point, because a small and roughly circular patch of the windowpane is clouded with fog.

She steps forward, hand outstretched. Presses her fingertips against the patch of fog. It's already fading. It might be her imagination, but it seems to her that she can feel faint warmth.

She glances around. She's in the bedroom. She doesn't remember coming in here. A single bedside lamp throwing the room into a sickly glow. There is suddenly nothing cozy or comfortable about any of this.

She's rushing as she leaves the room and goes to the back door, throws it open, and stares out into the night.

It's not silent. It never is. The soft calls of night birds, the constant creaking hum of the crickets. Wind in the trees. She stands motionless, hand on the doorframe, listening so hard that it's as though her very ears are vibrating.

But there's no strangeness in the forest, not that she can discern.

Something thin and hard clutched in her right hand. She looks at it, turns it over in the light from the back hall. That light gleams along the blade. At some point in her progress from bedroom to back door, she stopped off in the kitchen and picked up a knife. Yet another thing she doesn't recall doing, doesn't recall making the decision to do it.

She blinks. This is all extremely unsettling.

She descends the old steps, her bare feet swishing through the cool dew-damp grass. Passing a little way across the wide back lawn—still open although the forest understory is beginning to encroach—she pauses and turns, gazing at the house nestled into the night. Its lit windows look tiny and pitiful, like pointless defiance against something vast and inevitable.

At her back, through another screen of trees and down a small slope, is the lake.

If something came at her now, if it was smart about it, she would have only a very limited number of places she could run.

There's nothing out there.

Why should you believe that? Why should you be so certain?

Her attention flicks down to the knife in her hand. It's large. Heavy. She hefts it slightly and swallows. All at once the memory hits her, nearly hard enough to make her gasp: little girl in the house up north, the one she lived in when she still had two parents instead of one, and there was a cellar, an old one and poorly lit and smelling strongly of mildew and forgetting. Sent down there for something or other, she had been terrified of something unnameable and inexplicable and had desperately tried to find a way out of it, until finally dear old Dad lost his shit and threatened to hit her if she didn't go.

So when he wasn't looking, she grabbed a knife from the kitchen and hid it under her shirt. The metal was cold against the skin of her belly as she crept down the stairs. Climbing back up, she was absolutely positive that something was following her, something with vicious intent, and if she turned, she would see it, and even if she survived, she would never unsee it and would simply have to live in a world where such things were possible.

She ran, whatever she had been sent down there for in one hand and the knife in the other, and when she burst through the door and her father saw her holding it, she got hit anyway.

She wondered, after, whether he had ever in his life felt fear like that. She doubted it.

Now the urge to sprint back toward the house is almost overwhelming. She drags in a breath and struggles with it. If there's nothing out here, there's nothing to be afraid of.

But even now she's not so confident that there *wasn't* something following her up the cellar steps that day.

She takes another breath and walks to the left, passing around the side of the house in a wide arc. Searching the dark. Listening again. Walking as silently as she's able. The knife feels a little like the certainty she does not have.

Nothing.

But the bedroom is on the other side.

Around to the front, and past. She doesn't pause. It's brighter here, with the larger front windows and the lamps in the living room, and once again, she fights the urge to race for the door. She passes out of the light and back around, walking along the side of the flower beds. It occurs to her that she could have brought out a flashlight, should have, could still go back for one, but she doesn't turn around. Go back now and she might not return, but it's more than that.

If she turned on the steps and saw whatever was pursuing her, it couldn't be unseen.

She passes the bathroom window, reaches the bedroom, and halts. Stands, looking at the room through the glass; like she can now, anyone standing here could have been able to clearly see inside. Clearly see her.

She steps from the thick grass to the softer earth of the flower bed, pushes up on her toes and closely inspects the glass.

She sees nothing. Nothing of note. The window needs cleaning, all of them do, and there's a fine film of pollen all over everything; she's about to dismiss the whole thing when something catches her eye.

On the sill in that thin layer of pale yellow are some sweeping smears where the layer has been brushed away.

She looks at it for a while.

Doesn't have to mean anything. Could have been done by a bird, by a squirrel. Not at all what it looks like it might be, not at all by the human fingers of a human hand.

She's pulling away long before she actually steps back. The sensation of mental retreat is vaguely dizzying; she has enough distance on herself to grasp that it's happening, and that's as far as she cares to take it. This is an old practice by now, practically ritual: look away, turn away, and it will not have happened at all. Dismiss it and it's dismissed. But her feet press deeper into soft soil and before she can stop, she's bending, running her hands over it, over tufts of rogue grass and weeds and feeling for the dirt beneath.

Tracing unmistakable lines in an unmistakable shape.

She jerks her hand back. Ellis's fingertips grazing her knuckles. A spark like static and a tingle that lingers.

No, this is not like that.

She pushes abruptly upright and turns away, strides quickly back to the front door. The truth is that even if she wanted to entertain this any longer, what possible benefit is there in doing so out here? In the fucking dark?

It was just her own footprint, what she felt in the dirt beneath the window. She was walking all over the place, stepping everywhere. It was hers. That's all.

You were barefoot. It's her mother's voice, not faint and

quavery and insane like it was those last few times but instead affectionately tired with an edge of exasperation. *Sweetheart, did that feel like it came from a bare foot?*

Was it even your size?

In the front hall, in a patch of uneven shadow, she allows herself to fall back against the wall and sinks into her breathing. You make things normal by being normal in the midst of them. That's a lesson everyone had to learn on a whole new level. You make things normal by sheer force of will. You make things normal and then you don't have to be freaked out all the fucking time. And after a while, you could be amazed by how many things become normal, how many things you simply learn to accept and fold into what passes for your life.

She's not sure what shape the footprint was. She's not going back out there to look. It could be anything. It will remain Schrödinger's footprint.

She exhales and bends to brush dirt from the soles of her feet. She imagines that she can hear it land on the wood, soft as the whisper of snowfall.

The last two things that roll through her, in the mental cascade that exhausts her into sleep later on, are first that she can't remember how large Ellis's feet are.

The second is a question.

Were my eyes visible?

Did they see my eyes?

15

In the morning, everything looks the same, and every-thing has profoundly changed.

Fuck normal. She thinks it with a kind of hysterical giddiness entirely alien to her. Fuck normal. This is interesting. It's interesting, and in a far better sense of the word than most of the things that could have been called interesting in the last few years.

She has a neighbor.

She recalls that yesterday was weird and awkward and not remotely comfortable, yet those aspects of it have retreated into a vague background, and what she's recalling most vividly is the exhilaration of it, sitting in someone else's living room and drinking their tea and carrying on a conversation. Speaking of *normal*. How extraordinary it can become to hang out with someone.

Did she have fun? Is that the word for it? She isn't sure.

She does know that she wants to do it again. She wants it in a way seated far more in the body than anywhere else. She's jittery as she goes about her day; she needs to keep moving. Her belly flutters. Her feet itch, and she's positive that the itching would ease if she walked. Say, exactly the distance to Ellis's gate.

She won't.

Why the fuck not?

Because it's completely insane? Because doing it once was insane, and wasn't there something about how the blinders fell down and they both could have died?

So use the strap next time. Problem solved.

No, it is not.

She could drive herself well and truly crazy like this. She pulls on her boots and leaves the house in a stumbling rush, strides not toward the drive but in the opposite direction, toward the path that runs through the woods parallel to the lake. This is normal. This is the way she often goes. On the one hand, that means she doesn't have to think about where she's going; on the other, it means her mind is free to wander far afield all on its own.

What does she know about Ellis? What data has she collected thus far?

That Ellis lives reasonably close. That Ellis got there relatively recently. That Ellis's home is bright and simple. That Ellis used to be—still is?—a photographer.

Ellis's voice—that, she knows. She can call it up with ease. Smooth and low and slightly rough at the deeper edges, just a hint of vocal fry. For some reason, she thinks of it, and she thinks of a pair of hands, strong and calloused, and perhaps not especially graceful, but pleasant and warm to the touch. She thinks about a scattering of small white scars on the knuckles and backs of the fingers, nothing remarkable but merely the minor damage that one accumulates over years of use. Voices wear down in the same way. They change and are marked. We don't sound exactly the way we did five years ago.

And sometimes something smashes into us, does a lot

more than minor damage, and the changes are tremendous, and we listen to ourselves from the time Before and we no longer recognize what we hear.

Riley halts and stands in the center of the path, head cocked, listening. This time, she doesn't know for what. This time, she feels no fear.

She does feel the certainty that eyes are on her. Following her. Tracking.

An immense black flapping; she jumps, releases a little cry, and slaps her hands over her mouth as though she's done something to invite danger. A crow has alighted on a branch of the old beech just above and in front of her, and it regards her with cool, sharp eyes that put her in mind of something.

The photos yesterday. Ellis's photos. The eyes of the birds.

Riley swallows and meets the crow's gaze without flinching.

Making eye contact with lower-order animals was safe—they figured that out fairly quickly. But it never felt safe. Meeting the eyes of a pigeon, a dog being walked by an owner who beat an immediate and hasty retreat, a cat observing the world from its windowsill: all these encounters were accompanied by the thrill of doing something not only dangerous but forbidden. The violation of a taboo. Riley noted this feeling and was disturbed by it, and never mentioned it to anyone.

Increasingly, she wasn't mentioning anything to anyone. Mom died, and even with a few remaining friends online, she was alone. So at least it wasn't difficult to conceal a secret.

Now she meets the crow's eyes, and she's gratified

when it doesn't fly away. Crows are smart, she remembers. Smart enough to play games and use tools, and to remember human faces, to bear grudges, to warn other crows about whoever they bear the grudge against.

Is it possible they can also remember faces favorably?

Slowly, she raises a hand and gives it a little wave.

For a long moment, nothing. The crow doesn't move, barely twitches a feather. It merely stares at her, and gradually, it comes to her that she doesn't like that stare, doesn't like how it's holding itself, and also doesn't like the powerful sense that if she tried to pass beneath it and carry on down the path, something bad would happen.

She's scanning around for an option beyond just turning back and going home, when it launches itself at her.

A tight black arrow, wings folded against its sides; she sees it coming at her in a dark blur and throws her arms up in front of her face. Beak and talons. Something sharp raking down her bare forearms. *It's going for my eyes,* she thinks, with bizarre calm. *It's trying to put out my eyes.* Like the clawing nails of a human hand, that much force behind it—not a bird but some madman attempting to blind her with his bare hands.

It doesn't let up. She might be screaming. She beats furiously at the thing, as best she can without totally exposing her face, takes a stumbling step backward, teeters, tumbles onto her ass hard enough that her teeth clacking together sounds like a snapping bone. The crow follows her down, and it seems as if it's somehow multiplied itself— far too many wings fill her world, far too many beaks and angry caws.

Or those human hands again. Coming at her out of the dark, hissing and shrieking like a despairing banshee.

Giving her no choice. Her muscles lock up and shudder in a sudden convulsion, and she sees brilliant flashes of red on her hands, red pits gouged into her vision, and she thinks *I'm having a fucking seizure*.

And she thinks, insanely, *Mom, no.*

Blackness crowds in from all edges of her vision, swells and flows and covers everything.

It recedes, and she's kneeling in the dirt and gazing blankly down at the smashed body of the bird.

Her eyes flick to the rock clutched in her hand. Little larger than her fist. Glistening crimson, little pink flecks of flesh and dark spots of down. The crow's skull is caved in, but one eye is still locked onto her, unblinking, not wild and insane but cold and shining as a sheet of black ice. As if it didn't go mad at all but instead made a carefully calculated decision to attack.

She had no choice. She didn't. It made her do it. She didn't even mean to. Riley drags in a shaking breath and glances up and around, muscles vibrating in fine little tremors, the sharp tang of spent adrenaline on her tongue. She's scanning the trees, the branches, looking for more hunched black shapes, more shining eyes. Ready. Ready to do it again if she has to.

Could you?

Evidently.

Only dappled gold and green. Sun on the leaves.

She returns her focus to the bird. The single eye blinks, once, and then the shine dulls as the life evaporates from it.

Riley sets the stone down beside it with firm deliberateness and rocks back on her heels, clasping her blood-spattered hands in front of her. Trying not to focus on the crow and its destroyed body and its dull unblinking eye.

She has to think about this. There are any number of reasons why it might have done that. Her attention shifts to the scratches on her arms—nasty, though not so much as they might have been. It's amazing that she doesn't appear to be hurt anywhere else. Perhaps she is; perhaps she'll discover that when she gets home. Is she in danger of any kind of serious infection? At the very least, she should wash them out thoroughly when she's back, get some ointment on them.

She just beat an animal to death with a rock.

That she didn't mean to, that it was attacking her and she was merely defending herself does not alter that fact.

A couple of blows likely would have been sufficient to chase it off. *You smashed it into fucking paste. Just look at it.*

Riley has seen violence beyond what she once would have believed possible. She's seen gruesome, senseless murder. She's seen people destroying one another. Throats slashed, eyes gouged out, limbs severed, bodies crushed by vehicles and pulverized by falling. She's seen that a shotgun is capable of decapitation. She's seen several times just how much blood a human being contains. She should be past shock when it comes to this.

She rolls to the side, onto her hands and knees, and vomits up the morning's oatmeal in a heaving, scorching rush.

Somewhere above her, something screams.

How would I know? She wipes her mouth with the back of her shuddering hand, spitting bile. If it changed, if it mutated, if the rules were suddenly different, if they were wrong about the rules this whole time . . .

How the fuck would I know?

She could just look, is how.

She leaves the bird where it is. Kicks some leaves over it and over the rock, and feels more that she's trying to hide the evidence of a crime than give the animal any sort of final dignity. Or make it so that when she comes this way again, she'll be able to pass without having to look away from this spot—although she already knows she will.

She's okay. She's sane, and she's not dead. She doesn't have to worry, not about this, and she definitely doesn't have to feel guilty. She didn't do anything wrong; she didn't have a choice. It made her do it.

So she doesn't have to look. And she won't.

Back to the house. To the downstairs bathroom; she scrubs at the scratches harder than she needs to and hisses at the sting, rummages in the medicine cabinet; she did stock up on first aid when she originally came here, and she has more than enough in the way of antibacterial ointment and bandages.

Computer.

It won't turn on.

She sits in front of it, her finger hovering over the power button, and stares stupidly at the black cyclopean eye of the monitor.

The power isn't out. The fridge was humming when she passed through the kitchen. She presses the button again. For the hell of it, she clicks the mouse a few times and strikes some keys. The eye remains black. But it shows outlines, like the window did the night before. Objects. Walls. Her figure, sitting there and looking at it with unseen eyes.

Out of the depths of memory, an old chestnut from

the earlier days of tech support. *Did you check to see if it's plugged in?*

She scoots the chair back and slides under the desk, angles her head around to peer at the power strip and the back of the old tower.

It's plugged in, yes.

Every cable has been cut.

Not just the power cable. All of them. The mouse is optical, but the keyboard isn't, and that cable hasn't been spared. The cable that connects the monitor to the tower. Neatly cut, too; she touches one end, the fine little filaments of wire bound up in the casing. Clipped.

She scoots back and folds her knees up against her chest, wraps her bandaged arms around them. All at once, it's like she's back out in the woods, and the trees are full of silent crows, black feathery bodies packed together along every branch. Hundreds of them. Hundreds of pairs of cold eyes, gauging the angle of attack.

Just how deeply did you sleep last night?

Did you sleep at all?

Her cell phone is buried in the mud of the lake's bottom. She has no landline phone. Now this. Literally and figuratively cut off from the world outside what her own world has shrunk into.

I'm alone.

But she meets the monitor's cold, black, dead eye, and she knows that isn't true.

16

Riley didn't sleepwalk as a child, or an adult of the younger variety. But then, after, she did.

Never far. There wasn't far to go. But night after night, with increasing frequency: rising out of unconsciousness like struggling out of thick tarry water, finding herself in the middle of her tiny living room. At the window. Facing her kitchen sink. In the bathroom, looking at where her mirror once was. No memory whatsoever of how she got there. No memory of anything whatsoever. Not even dreams.

Thinking: *This is a trauma response. It's perfectly natural.* Didn't feel natural.

She wondered if her eyes were open when she walked as she slept. What would happen if she somehow encountered an unprotected face? Would a lack of consciousness be enough to shield her? Does it count as not seeing, if you aren't aware of what you see?

The creeping temptation to make the experiment. Only no real practical way to do that.

Her apartment was only a couple of hundred feet square. Not much room to wander. The frankly disturbing image of her walking in tight, ponderous circles, going nowhere and gazing at nothing. It wasn't something she especially cared to see, but one night, she recorded herself anyway, set up a cam in her living room and checked it in the morning. It was a shitty old cam, and the night vision function was quite bad—fortunate, maybe, rendering eyes nothing but dark blurs—but she saw enough.

No wandering. She came walking dreamily into the room and stopped, turned, stared directly at the camera.

She stayed like that for a good half hour. Then exited the frame, back toward the bedroom.

Only after she stopped the playback did it occur to her that she had been looking at her own face. The resolution was not much better than the night vision, and her eyes had been little more than indistinct spots, but she had been looking nonetheless.

She had been looking and she felt okay, long after the point at which she should have been dead if anything was going to happen.

It wasn't her main takeaway, but it was one of them: do not ever assume that you will be okay next time merely because you were this time.

Her main takeaway was that she wasn't going to film herself again. If she got hurt sleepwalking, she'd deal with that as it came. Otherwise she was going to let it go. Otherwise she wasn't going to think about it anymore. It wasn't as though she could really do anything about it. Anyway, it also wasn't as though she seemed to be doing anything but walking and standing.

Not breaking anything. Cutting anything up.

She stopped doing it after a few more months.

She's pretty sure about that.

17

"Holy shit, what the hell happened to you?"

Ellis sounds more bewildered than alarmed, but the alarm is there, and Riley wonders what she looks like. Her arms are definitely a sight, some of the deeper scratches still bandaged a day later and some open to the air and scabbed over. Not too bad. Not as bad as when she got them. But how they look to you isn't always a reliable guide to how others will take them.

She's wearing her blinders. She called out as she came up the drive, and Ellis called back; with one of them protected, they should both be all right, but Ellis will be careful in any case. You learn how to look at someone without ever lifting your eyes above their chest.

It's not any kind of sure thing, but you learn.

Riley shrugs. She had time to come up with an explanation and she didn't, and she suspects that only part of that is that the truth is impossible to really explain in any way that doesn't make it sound at least a little bit insane. So she could lie. But the world has gone insane, so likely it's a stupid thing to worry about.

Whole thing still feels distinctly unreal anyway.

"Got attacked by a bird," she says simply and shrugs

again, shifts from foot to foot on the gravel. She hears the creak of the steps, the sound of Ellis slowly coming toward her, and she self-consciously rubs at her arms. Should have worn a jacket or something, maybe. But the day is hot.

"Seriously?" Ellis exhales. "What did you do, insult its mother?"

Riley laughs. It startles her, the volume and the uncharacteristically shrill edge. But it's funny. Whole thing is vaguely comical. Better to recognize that, keep it all from getting too brittle.

"I didn't do anything. I just went for a fucking walk."

"Maybe you went too close to its nest or something."

"Yeah," Riley murmurs. "Maybe." What she won't talk about is how the thing looked at her, the cold calculation she saw in its gaze, how it didn't hesitate when it flew at her, how it clearly would have killed her if it could, and indeed, it did seem to be putting in a fair effort.

She also won't talk about the bloody rock in her hands and the crushed body on the ground in front of her. That won't make any of this any less awkward, she thinks.

Might make her less desirable company.

But also, it hits her that this is comforting, because it's independent confirmation that it happened at all.

"Should you have gone to a hospital? Could be it was sick or something." Pause. Hospitals. Do those even exist anymore? "I don't think birds carry rabies, right?"

"Don't think they do, no." Do they? She could check. Or—

No, she can't check.

She sucks in a breath, stops herself from picking at

the peeling edge of one of the bandages. "Do you have a computer?"

"No." Quizzical. "I didn't bring it with me. Honestly, I didn't want to have one. Maybe the same reason you tossed your phone."

"What about a phone?"

"I have an Android thing. It's like a hundred years old, but it still works okay. You—" The pause is longer, and heavy. Ellis sounds fairly close now, perhaps only a few feet away, and with vivid inner vision, Riley can just about perceive the troubled understanding spreading across a face she's never seen. "You don't have any way to contact anyone. Do you?"

Riley shakes her head. "Not anymore."

She hopes, very much, that now that she's been foolish enough to open this topic, the subject of her own computer won't enter the frame.

Ellis exhales again. Says nothing. The silence stretches out, and Riley fights the impulse to squirm, to cast about for something else to say. She allows it to cover her, feels the sunshine on her face and bare arms, and the pressure of Ellis's focus on her.

She does not understand why this person pushes her so firmly onto the wrong feet. Perhaps, after all this time alone, anyone would.

Perhaps not.

At last, Ellis walks past her, a shadow moving in a world of shadows. "Go for a walk with me?" Beat, then: "If we go single file and I don't turn around, let you know anytime I'm going in a different direction, we should be fine."

If is doing some work there. Because you can take precautions and it can end up still not being enough. She's heard about it.

She's seen it.

But she doesn't surprise herself much when she turns and starts to follow, and hooks her thumbs into the straps of her blinders, tugs them up on her forehead like a pair of aviator goggles.

"Okay. Sure."

18

The path that Riley usually takes is not confined to her property or even the undeveloped forest immediately surrounding it. It's a hiking trail that runs all around the lake, snaking through the trees and dipping around private plots, running close to the bank before climbing up to proceed along a ridge. It's a nice path, not overly strenuous but intense enough to make you feel accomplished if you make it around the whole loop.

Riley has taken the whole loop countless times now.

The terrain is relatively flat here, winding through a broad stand of pines, and Riley follows Ellis, hands in the pockets of her jeans. The path itself is eroded to the point that roots crisscross it and make the going a bit treacherous, and Riley has to keep over half her attention on the ground in front of her. But also she sees Ellis in the upper periphery of her vision, and she can't stop looking. She's fascinated. It's fascinating.

It's more of Ellis than she's had a chance to get a real good look at since they met.

Powerful, slightly stocky legs in jeans darker and more worn than hers. Slim hips. A thick brown leather belt with a complex yet subtle plait design etched into it. The hem of a gray tee. The lower dip of a broad back.

She doesn't dare go higher.

She could, she thinks. She could, just for a few seconds, and it would almost certainly be fine. Ellis knows the danger of turning, at least turning without announcing the turn. But the path is a trip-fest. What if Ellis's boots got snagged and those powerful legs crumpled? What if there was a turn that happened too quickly to announce?

People hoped that infection—for lack of any better way to think about it—required a longer exposure. But it didn't. It doesn't. At least not always. A glimpse might be enough.

She could go higher. She could. It repeats over and over between her ears with the expansion and contraction of her lungs, the flutter of her pulse. Just a peek. It would be safe enough.

No, it wouldn't, and you fucking know it.

"I think I get why you did it," Ellis says, voice raised above a sudden gust of wind that shakes the treetops and sets them whispering. "Ditched the phone. Why you don't have a computer. Used to be we basically couldn't live without those fucking things, right?" Huffed laugh. "But I remember when people started shutting it all off. Just . . . pulled into themselves. I didn't do it myself, but I knew people who did."

"Yeah," Riley murmurs. Her focus has returned fully to the path, the chaotic network of roots.

The computer.

"I don't know," Ellis adds, "how you're expecting to get any supplies out here now—but you don't have to explain it. But I'd bet you didn't actually think it through. You get this far and after a while it's like you just d—"

"It's like you just do things," Riley cuts in quietly.

Like you sabotage your own last safe link to the outside and you don't remember doing it.

"Right. You do stuff and you don't always even know why." Ellis neatly steps over a thick branch, the ends dead and splintered and pale. "You can use my phone, y'know. If you need to order things." Thin amusement. "I don't want you to starve."

"Thanks," Riley says—still a murmur. Nothing about the stock of food she already has, that she should be all right for a while yet. Nothing about how this is something she actually didn't intend at all, on any level, and one of the strangest things about it might be that she feels almost no fear at all. Merely a kind of absent bemusement.

Nothing about the computer. The cables.

If she talks about that, then it becomes something worth talking about.

"I like these woods," Ellis says, lower. Slower pace, as if taking the time to really draw it all in. "This trail. Didn't have this where I came from."

"Where did you come from?"

"Oh." Vague tone. Notably. The audible equivalent of a wave of the hand. "I told you, remember? Gated community, just this place in the suburbs. Like anywhere. Nothing remarkable about it."

Yes, she does remember now. She remembers that it was allegedly ugly.

A rustle-crash in the trees off to the left. Riley doesn't pause, but she turns her head, peering. Deer, sounds like.

They're thick in here. Practically an infestation, albeit a pretty one.

"Why'd you leave?"

"I didn't tell you?"

Riley returns her gaze to the ground. The roots over which she's stepping are worn, almost polished, as if from the passage of many feet. "Let's say you didn't."

"I just wanted to get away from it," Ellis says simply. "There were a lot of rules. They were supposed to be for everyone's protection, and I guess they were, but . . ."

Trailing off, and for a moment, only the dry thump of their footfalls and the buzz of insects, the latter rising in volume as the day warms.

"It wasn't that I thought there shouldn't be rules," Ellis says finally, carefully. "I just . . . I got to the point where I needed to get out. I needed to go somewhere where I felt freer, where I was totally alone. That's all."

"You aren't totally alone, though," Riley points out, and Ellis laughs.

"No, I guess I'm not. How about that. Oh," Ellis adds. The blur of an arm, gesturing. "There's the lake."

There's the lake. Shimmering through the trees, rippling around the roots of the ones growing out of the bank and directly into the water. Ellis turns off the trail and starts down a small gully, using saplings as handholds when the dirt starts to slide, and Riley follows.

But not immediately.

She doesn't have to give it much thought, when she steps forward and angles herself so that she can't glimpse Ellis's face even in profile. Still, she catches a glimpse of the back and part of the side of Ellis's head: short-cropped black hair streaked with silver, a freckled nape, the outline of a strong jaw's hinge. Right ear, line of plain silver studs proceeding up the cartilage. They shine like the water.

She wants to touch the studs. Lay her fingertip against each one. Her own ears are pierced—once, sensibly in the lobe—but she can't recall when she last bothered wearing anything in them. So this would be a novelty. Something else crashing through the monotony, even if very small.

It isn't until she's standing behind Ellis on the bank and gazing out at the water that she realizes what it is that's just happened.

Ellis said Riley would be informed of any course change well ahead of time. But that isn't how it went. Ellis merely made a choice, and Riley had to adjust. And she did, not with any particular difficulty, but—

But there might have been difficulty.

She fingers the band of her blinders just above her ear. The pressure is beginning to call up the most distant rumbles of a headache.

Your new friend just put you in danger. How do you feel about that? Do you think it was intentional? Or was it in-difference?

She still really doesn't know Ellis at all.

Ellis points to the far bank, the white edge of a house. A dark roof. A dock, with no boat visible. "You ever see other people out here?"

"That specific house? Or just in general?"

Ellis rolls a shoulder. "Just in general. This seems like a place people would make full use of when they could, so, y'know, it also seems like a place people might run to. Get brave after a while and start doing things like fishing and going swimming."

"I haven't seen anything like that in a long time," Riley says softly. "Now and then, I see a light." Beat. She frowns. Something about how Ellis said *seems like*. "Did you come out here a lot, Before?"

"Huh?" Ellis sounds honestly confused.

"Didn't you say it was your parents' vacation house? Did you ever come out here with them?"

"No." Throat cleared, a bit rough-sounding. Riley is having to fight to keep her gaze from fixing once more on the back of Ellis's head. "They got it recently. That is—not too long before everything happened. I never got a chance."

"And then they died?"

"Yes," Ellis says, with just a hint of tension. "Then they died."

How? It's not her fucking business, she supposes, but she can guess at any number of possible ways. The worst is if they killed each other, she thinks. *Please let that not be what happened.* Strange to care about this person, maybe, when she hardly knows Ellis at all and not caring much about people long ago became a survival skill, but she hopes that it wasn't that. She hopes that's not what Ellis is carrying around.

Except that's the most likely possibility. That's how it often went. It was the people closest to you who did it. Or you did it to them. Or, in a perverse mutuality, you simultaneously did it to each other.

There's a reason—really, many reasons—why the birth rate had dropped to virtually nothing the last time she cared to check. Which was a long time ago, but still.

"My mom died," she murmurs, and stops, amazed at herself—amazed and a little appalled.

That was not planned. That was not said with her express consent.

The silence is dense. She can feel Ellis listening. Looks at those strong shoulders and imagines that she can see it in the set of the muscles.

"How bad was it?"

Somehow she admires whatever courage prompted Ellis to be so direct. Then again, perhaps such directness is what happens to some people when they spend enough time alone.

She doesn't have a lot to compare it to.

She shrugs, remembers that Ellis can't see her, feels a warm, small flush of embarrassment. "Not really that bad." She chews her bottom lip. "She killed herself. It wasn't infection or anything," she adds. "I think she was pretty far gone in her own way by the end, but she was definitely still—"

"She was still her," Ellis finishes.

"Yeah."

"I could never decide if that was better." Ellis steps forward, hands in pockets, shoes squishing in the wetter ground just above where the water touches it. "Which is weird, because of course on paper it's better. To go as yourself, to have hold of that much of you before you stopped existing at all, or to not have any idea it was happening."

"You think they don't have any idea?"

No one knows. No one has ever been in a position to ask. The few attempts to take an infected person into some form of custody never ended well. Riley remembers. Saw it, once—footage of it leaked onto the net. A teenage girl, apparently infected and sedated, going into sudden convulsions, dead with a mouth full of bloody foam barely seconds later. *Massive organ failure,* they said.

Not the ugliest thing she ever saw in those early months, but it's stayed with her the way few other things have.

"I hope they don't," Ellis says. "I hope they don't know what's happening to them. I hope your brain just breaks in an instant and it's like you're already gone. I mean, imagine the alternative. Imagine being aware of all of it as it happens. As you . . . do whatever you do." Pause. "I honestly can't think of anything worse."

"That's one of those things I usually try not to think about." Riley is beginning to wish she hadn't said anything at all. "Anyway, yeah, she killed herself, and in a way, it was almost better, because at least I didn't have to worry about her anymore."

Worrying about her all alone in a house of broken glass, with her empty eye sockets healing raw and badly in her face.

"Did you ever think about doing it?"

There's a twitch in Ellis's shoulder and side that is so minute, so brief, it would be easy to miss or to not interpret at all. But Riley doesn't miss it. And she doesn't fail to interpret it.

Ellis almost turned around to look at her. For a split second. Almost.

Aware of it? Or not?

She licks her lips. When she speaks, it comes out in a croak. "Doing what?"

But she knows perfectly well *what.*

"Taking yourself out of the equation. Taking care of it first before anyone else can."

Riley senses that it isn't squeamishness keeping Ellis from merely saying *killing yourself*. It's more that *killing yourself*, while technically correct, captures none of the totally sensible logic of that decision. *Taking care of it* sounds rational. *Killing yourself* does not.

Anyway, there's yet again no reason to not answer the question honestly.

"Of course I did."

"You didn't go through with it, though," Ellis observes with a touch of wry humor, and goes on before Riley can respond: "I remember when it started really happening. Like it was more than a few here and there. Whole families. And like . . ." Sharp sigh. Ellis bends, picks up a stone from the mud, hurls it into the water with a soft *splosh*. "Normally, I would've been pissed off about that. About when it was families. Who does that? Who has the fucking right? But I wasn't pissed off. I didn't feel—"

"Didn't feel much of anything. I know."

"You get it, how someone can love someone else to where that—where doing it peacefully, painlessly—seems like the best option. Because you can't bear to watch the worst happen to them. Much less *be* the worst that happens. And you feel like it's just a matter of time before it does." Ellis pauses a few seconds. "In any case, I did, too. I guess probably all of us did."

Like a singular moment of decision shared by all humanity. Opt out, or keep trying to make it work? For once, judgment was pointless. No one was truly in a position to do the judging. Only it wasn't a singular moment but a series of moments, repeating every day, making every second of every day another point of decision.

Technically, she could still do it anytime. Given that

there's no one to find her and call an ambulance, it might be easier than ever.

But there is someone now.

Riley clears her throat again, shifts from foot to foot. There's a tightness about the set of Ellis's shoulders now, and it's doing something to Riley's diaphragm that she doesn't know how to describe. "Do you want to keep going? Head back?"

Ellis breathes a laugh. "You got somewhere to be?"

"No, I just—" Flustered now. She doesn't like it. "I dunno, I—"

"Hey, it's fine. Sorry I was getting morbid." Shake of the shoulders and the tightness disappears. "You should probably turn around."

Riley is about to ask why, when she gets it. Of course. She turns, feeling like an idiot and therefore even more flustered, and starts to make her way back up the slope, the dry crunch of Ellis's shoes very loud in her ears as overhead the bird calls echo through the branches.

19

"So your place is like this one?"

Ellis has a deck. It's a small one, and like the inside of the house it's plain and comfortable. Couple of chairs, a table with an umbrella. The canvas-covered hulk of what must be a grill. They're sitting on it, both with blinders on now, gazing through the trees at a brilliant sunset visible only as a dull, sullen glow. The evening is warm, and the can of beer is sweating into Riley's hand, its hoppy bitterness sharp on her tongue. There is still beer. Somehow, there is still beer, just as somehow there are still many things from Before.

Once she would have enjoyed this immensely. Now she's not certain what she feels.

"Mostly." She shrugs—which might or might not be visible—and takes another swallow. "The inside isn't as nice. I don't have a deck."

"Well, you can use this one if you want. Just give me a heads-up."

"How? I don't have a phone."

Ellis laughs quietly. "Smoke signals? Maybe you can make a really loud noise. Do you have an air horn or something?"

It sounds like a joke, but it's actually a pretty good idea. Riley's brow furrows as she combs through what vague inventory of her belongings she carries around with her. "I'm not sure. Let me dig through the basement. There's all kinds of crap down there."

"I'd like to see your place sometime. Deck or no deck."

It's said offhand, casual, in the way that someone tosses something out there without any expectation that it'll be picked up. But Riley stiffens, her eyes darting in Ellis's direction although Ellis isn't any less of a shapeless hulk than the grill. Why should that suggestion get this kind of reaction out of her? Ellis has been perfectly hospitable. Why shouldn't Riley reciprocate? How would that not be the most basic courtesy?

And yet.

You've been alone for such a long time. Of course you're balking. It's okay.

"Yeah," she says, sounding appropriately noncommittal. In times Before, there were any number of excuses she might have come up with to not have people over. A bathroom in which she'd been endlessly postponing doing a deep clean. An infestation of ants. A broken AC. The lack of those excuses is a kind of troubling defenselessness. "Sometime, sure."

There's a wide, unmissable bloodstain on her floor.

Of course, Ellis might see it and simply never remark.

These days, it may even be unremarkable.

A movement against the lighter sky—a beer lifted in a toast. "To sometime," Ellis says, and it sounds only a little bit like mockery.

20

Later, in the broken darkness of a high and nearly full moon, Riley sits on the bare floor where the desk used to be and stares at the clipped cables in her hands as if she still doesn't totally understand them.

No big deal, she thought for a hot minute, just order some new ones—hell, order a whole damn new computer, and then it hit her, how impossible it is for her to do that now, at least without outside assistance, and she laid her head on her bent knees and laughed.

She could, if she were so inclined, go to Ellis and explain the whole situation and ask for that assistance. Hell, she could probably avoid the explanation. Merely ask for assistance with the ordering part and let the rest be.

But if she does that—if she acknowledges what's happened even to that degree, if she cracks the door open even that much—it leaves this room. If it leaves this room, it can't be put away again. It and everything it is, everything it implies—it becomes real, it must be dealt with in all its reality, and Riley thinks of the cold beer delightful in her hand and Ellis's magnetic, unsettling company, and it all just seems like a little more reality than she's equipped to handle. Outside this room, it's remote and easy to disregard. Outside this room, it's not a big deal. It's just one of those things. Shit happens. Et cetera.

Inside this room, she can hold the cables and look at them and feel her brain spitting sparks as it struggles to grind through what it could mean.

Can being alone this long make you stupid? It can certainly make you crazy. Or she imagines it can. She's heard of such things. She used to live in terror of insanity, because no longer being able to trust your own perception struck her as one of the worst fates imaginable. But then it started happening all the time to everyone, and perversely, that removed its fangs rather than lengthening and sharpening them. You can't ever really trust yourself anyway. Not when you get right down to it. There's always doubt. You know you're fucked up when there isn't. You know you've lost it when you think you have the firmest hold.

She runs her thumb over the tops of the cut cables. The light prickle of the wires protruding from their casings. The cut was not merely neat, it was assured. A single motion, done by someone who was in absolutely no doubt about what they wanted to do.

She threw her phone away. Wasn't this the logical next step?

What were *you trying to do?*

In all of this, what are you trying to do?

Riley throws the cables against the wall and draws her knees up again, wraps her arms around them. Rocking back and forth feels like it might be a bridge too far in the direction of crazy, even for her and even for now, so she avoids it. She merely sits, staring at her own shadow hunched beneath the windowsill like an observing ghost.

It vanishes as the light cuts out.

She doesn't jump. Doesn't even twitch. This happens so frequently now. Anyway, there isn't a significant difference in this moment between the darkness and the light. This way, she doesn't have to see anything; the moon is casting its light on the other side of the house, and all she receives where she is now is a residual, bloodless glow. Far too weak to see anything by.

Might as well go the fuck to bed. She gets slowly to her feet, starts to turn—freezes.

Stares out the window at the narrow stretch of grass below.

Shadows on shadows can be difficult to parse. But she's had practice. Perceiving the world through glasses colored not rose but ink, she's learned to read minute degrees of shadow, like a creature long-lived underground. Now she looks out into the endlessly fine gradations of shadow delineated only by the faintest illumination, reflected light of reflected light, and she cannot tell herself that she doesn't see the human shape standing there in the grass.

She can tell nothing about it other than that it's human. Can't tell for certain its height. What it's wearing. It has no features. But she can feel its eyes on her—or she imagines she can, seconds before it hits her that the lights in here are off and it's entirely possible she's even less visible than it is.

But her face might be framed in the window. The hint of a ghost of a darkened moon.

Slowly, birdlike, the figure cocks its head.

Two things happen, and she's never sure which one actually did.

She plunges through the door and tears down the stairs, bare feet thundering against the thin carpet over the wood, and she veers through the kitchen and only just catches herself on the island before she goes sprawling, half falls against the kitchen counter and snatches up a knife from the block, slams through the back door, and pounds into the grass with the blade a dancing gleam in the lower periphery of her vision. The grass is slimy between her toes, licks at her ankles like cold, wet tongues. She rounds the side of the house and skids to a halt, gasping, one hand braced against her upper thigh and the other gripping the knife, staring at the place in the grass where nothing but the grass now is.

She slowly turns away from the window and walks, one deliberate step at a time, to her bed. Tugs off her sweatpants and climbs in beneath the covers, curls in on herself like she remembers doing when she was a little girl after a particularly bad day. Mom's fingers stroking through her hair. Telling her she was fine, everyone has bad days, everything would be fine. Riley runs her hands over her bare shins, and shapes flit through her mind, fluttering like moths behind her closing eyelids.

It's all shapes. It doesn't matter what you see. It's all just moving shapes in still light. That's all it's ever been.

21

I'd love to see you sometime, Ellis says, and Riley says nothing. She sips her beer, looks out over the shadows that are the trees and the water and the sky. It's amazing—although perhaps it shouldn't be—how swiftly she stopped being bothered by blinders. How easy it was to make it normal to herself. She's gotten very good at making things normal to herself, and that was true before the world broke apart and changed.

Movement to her right. The sound of aluminum on plastic, the tiny hiss of bubbles. Shoes against boards. Distant wings. Ellis is getting up. She knows this without turning her head: Ellis is getting up, and Ellis is coming toward her, stopping in front of her and blotting out the shadows that are the trees and the water and the sky with a black nothingness, a person-shaped hole in the world. Riley looks up at it, at Ellis, and the can in her hand seems to get colder as Ellis bends toward her and curls gentle fingers around the straps of the blinders and lifts them away from Riley's eyes.

She should close her eyes. Now, immediately. Before it's too late.

She does not do that. She blinks owlishly in the lowering sun and looks up, her breath as still as light in her chest.

"Hi," Ellis says, and Ellis's voice is rough and hoarse in a way it wasn't before. A grating throat-caw. Ellis's voice has never been like that. That isn't right. Riley frowns. She is meeting Ellis's eyes.

There is something wrong with Ellis's eyes.

With one of them. One is normal. What color? She can't tell for some reason, but she knows there's nothing wrong with it. But the other one seems larger than the first, and its surface is moving very slightly. Flexing. Bulging unevenly this way and that. Something glitters in the black circle of pupil.

"Hi," Riley breathes.

"Nice to finally meet you," Ellis says, and a wickedly curved black beak stabs through the pupil and tears past the cornea in a burst of inky fluid that streams over Ellis's grinning teeth, stretches wide in a furiously silent scream. A cold, murderous eye peers out from the ruins and fixes Riley's. Riley's own scream is anything but silent. Ellis's mouth opens and releases a torrent of mocking cries and a chaos of wings.

22

Riley checks the back door. It's closed, locked. She checks the knife block. All present and correct. She examines her feet. No flecks of grass or leaves stuck to the skin.

She wonders dimly if any of that should—*could*—ever be enough.

23

"Do you ever see anyone around here?"

Riley makes the question casual. She doesn't have to try very hard. It's two days later. There have been no unexplained shapes and no dreams. What is in that room will stay in that room, because she has decided that it will.

From behind her, Ellis huffs a laugh. "Sure, I'm seeing you right now."

Riley rises from the love seat, turns—not in any direction that would bring her face-to-face with Ellis. Not even a glimpse. Not long in each other's presence, not much time to learn each other's rhythms, and they've already started internalizing how to instinctively keep out of each other's line of sight. They're back in Ellis's bright living room, and now Riley is idly scanning one of the bookshelves, making a survey of the titles. Mostly nonfiction: some stuff on photography, ancient history, a few long but clearly popular-oriented ecology texts. One shelf of what Riley imagines would be considered *classic* novels. *Frankenstein. Bleak House. Gulliver's Travels. Heart of Darkness. The Grapes of Wrath.*

It hits her suddenly, how little personality there is in

these books. How nondescript they are. Might see them anywhere.

"I don't mean me," she says a little absently. As if she doesn't know it was a joke. "I mean other people."

"I haven't been here that long." Sip. Not beer this time; iced tea, unsweetened. "You've been here way longer than me. You said you didn't see people much, I thought."

"Lights," Riley murmurs. Lights might be anything, mightn't they? "I mean closer up than that."

"I haven't seen anyone," Ellis says quietly. Then: "Why?"

Riley shrugs. "No reason. Guess I just wondered if anyone else had come to check out the new neighbor."

"I haven't seen anyone except you." Beat of silence. "Honestly, I like it that way."

"How come?"

"I like being around you," Ellis says, still quiet. It does sound as if Ellis is closer. But the room plays oddly with echoes and it's difficult to tell. "I don't know when I last liked being around anyone."

Riley pulls in a slow breath, her fingers resting motionless against the glass curve. "Why do you like being around me?"

"I dunno. I get the sense that you're not high-maintenance, for one. Don't get me wrong, you're kind of weird." Wry amusement. "But like you said, aren't we all?"

Riley laughs softly, sets down the ornament. But the laugh doesn't seem to reach down further into her than her throat. There's something about this that has her feeling jumpy, fidgety, and it's not the sort of environmental unease she felt at first. It may have something to do with how she can't tell how close Ellis is. How that uncertainty is lifting the hair on the back of her neck, making her want to turn suddenly.

It's not paranoia. She doesn't think. She's not sure what the hell it is.

"I pretty much always lived alone," she says instead and continues her slow circuit of the room. Windows, grass, trees. The view at least is virtually identical. If she focuses on it, she might convince herself that she never ventured away from what has been her center of safety and familiarity for years now. Has been until recently. "How about you?"

Ellis doesn't answer right away. Once again, Riley pulls to a stop, one hand on the folds of the open blinds, and listens to that silence. Parses the quality of it. There could be any number of reasons for Ellis to hesitate.

Pain, for one.

"I lived with—with someone," Ellis says finally, carefully. "For a while."

For a while. So there was an end point. There were a lot of those.

"Was it the outbreak?"

Silence again. Then: "Not . . . exactly. I just stopped. Living with them. No, they didn't die," Ellis goes on before Riley can ask. "I just didn't want to do it anymore."

Riley swallows. This, too, was such a common story: if people didn't kill one another, they voluntarily parted ways. Or sometimes only half voluntarily. They broke apart—out of terror. Out of despair. Out of love. So many people, all left alone. "Was it hard?"

"It was the hardest thing I've ever done," Ellis says softly, and the ache in those words, pain dense and cold as lead, is almost too much to bear.

And suddenly, Riley doesn't want to ask anymore. Suddenly the urge to turn is back, and it's kind of overwhelming. She wants to turn around and locate Ellis in this unfamiliar territory, approach, reach out, and—

And what?

"I'm sorry," Riley whispers. She sees her own reflection then, a featureless ghost superimposed over shades of sunlit green.

"Don't be. It was for the best in the end." Roughly cleared throat. "Anyway, it took me a while to get back on my feet again, but I did. I made it." Once again, that wry amusement. "Was a little touch-and-go for a bit there, but yeah. Here we are."

"You were lucky," Ellis says after another moment or two. Definitely closer now. Riley feels a twitch of what might be alarm. It's dangerous to move like that, without announcing the movement to the other party, without signaling your position relative to them. It invites an accident. "You must've thought that more than once. I'm telling you, you were. It was always easier to have nothing to lose."

"What about now?"

"What about now?" Ellis sounds mildly confused.

"I'm in your house," Riley murmurs. "And you said you like being around me."

"Oh."

It sounds as if Ellis is directly at her shoulder. Very close. She heard no footsteps. She received no warning. She should be furious, she thinks. She should be incensed at the danger they might both be in now, that Ellis might have put them in. But she feels nothing of the kind. Instead, she's suffused with that prickle, the sensation of hormone rush. What chemicals does the body release upon the event of proximity? *This isn't right,* she thinks. *This just isn't right.*

Heat races across her skin.

"Do you need some kind of proof?" Ellis asks, quiet. Low and bemused.

Riley says nothing. Swallows. The silence hangs in the air between them, taut as a fishing line onto which something has been hooked. Suddenly, crazily, anger pervades the already present heat, flushes up her spine and into her ears, pulsing hot and red. Surely visible, if Ellis is looking. How would that redness be interpreted? How many ways can a blush be read?

This isn't fair, is what she thinks in the red haze of that strange anger. She's being jerked around. Played with. It's not fair, and she hates it.

She drags in a slow breath, lays her hand flat against the windowpane, notes the almost imperceptible outline of fog spreading outward from her warmth, and at the same instant, warm breath puffing against the outer shell of her ear and the nape of her neck, and her teeth snap down on her lower lip in an instinctive bid to stifle her moan as something more concrete than breath grazes her skin.

Lips. It's been a very long time, but you don't forget the feeling of lips stirring the fine down just below your hairline. Pressing. Not a kiss. Far too exploratory for that. Asking a kind of permission to proceed.

Just where the fuck do you think you're going?

There's a place she knows well, wherein anger and terror mix and intertwine in furiously sensuous union until one can no longer separate the two and it's a kind of madness in and of itself, dangerous because thinking is not part of it, because it makes you its own sort of crazy and you make mistakes that lead to far worse things than mere everyday insanity. Ellis's barely there touch shoves Riley into it now, and she whips her head forward and smashes it into the window with all her strength, the glass shattering and showering and ringing tunefully off the bare floor and blood pours hot and coppery into her mouth.

No. She doesn't do that. She goes rigid, fingers clenching, and the warmth and the contact behind her is gone so suddenly she can almost believe it was never there.

Are you really sure it was?

But Ellis's voice, when it comes, is shaking. Not much, but Riley does notice it. A few feet away, sounds like. Perhaps from the sofa.

"I'm sorry."

"Don't," Riley mutters. She doesn't know what *don't* refers to in this case; that ambiguity might actually be a plus. *Don't apologize. Don't you fucking dare do that again. Don't you fucking dare stop.*

Or maybe to herself: *Don't think. Don't think about what almost just happened. Don't think about what you might have done.*

Don't think about what you want.

"It's getting late," Ellis says softly after another moment. "You should probably get back."

"Yes."

Ellis says nothing else. Riley turns in a cautious arc, locks her gaze onto the wall, and passes into the front hall, keeps her gait steady, lays her hand on the screen door's handle. Outside, the oncoming dusk. Really, it is better if she leaves now. Better that she not be walking home in the dark. Better—because it just is, that's all.

Sudden movement behind her, and her hand freezes. All of her freezes, the heat draining away, an awful cold blankness left behind. Not very distant from paralysis.

It's difficult to imagine what she might do now, but she's cognizant that a reasonable person would probably bolt.

She does nothing of the kind. She stands in this frozen patch of nothing and misses the anger, because the anger was active. The anger felt like agency, not like being swept along by something under no control of her own. She thinks of roller coasters. It's been close to a decade since she was last on one, rising and rising and then falling and falling and falling and screaming ecstatic fear as she falls. Do they even exist anymore?

Does anything outside this house exist?

Something brushes the back of her hand, so quick and so light that it might not have happened at all.

"Good night," Ellis says quietly, and Riley opens the door and steps out onto the porch.

It's not night. It's not even getting dark yet. But it's coming. She feels it far more than sees it, like a change in air pressure announcing a storm. It's coming, and there's nothing she can do to stop it.

She walks down the steps, but doesn't head out on the gravel drive; she turns toward the tree line, the pale cord of the path snaking off through the shadows of the trunks. It's a longer way. She'll have more time to think. About something. About nothing. About whatever.

"Good night," Ellis repeats behind her, so low and quiet as to be on the verge of inaudible. "Sweet dreams."

24

All the way home through the woods, she's expecting to sense someone following her. A shadow flitting between the trees. The crackle of broken twigs. A rustle of leaves. A footstep behind her.

Nothing happens. The woods are quiet—except for the crows crying above her as they fly ahead, like harbingers warning of her coming.

Hypervigilance. That's the word, she's almost sure of it. So keenly aware of everything that it's bordering on pathological, so focused on sensory input that one might begin to perceive patterns that aren't even there, signals in the noise, like how voices can emerge from the sound of a fan or an air conditioner. You can never quite make out what they're saying but it's so clear, so undeniable, and it's not real.

You might feel a little like you're going crazy.

But as she proceeds along the path, she feels herself being drawn back, back to Ellis's house, back to that moment by the window, when something almost happened.

And what something was that?

Was it Ellis, was it what Ellis might have done, what

she might have done with Ellis, a heady and marrow-watery chaos of images and sensations?

Or was it her slamming her head against the window, slashing her forehead open, pale pink flash of bone beneath the shredded flesh and all that blood in her mouth?

She doesn't know when she last had a thought like that.

She has, though. Doesn't everyone? Flashes of intrusion from a deeper and deeply chaotic self, concealed so well most of the time but occasionally fighting its way free and sending up an unsummoned thought. The worst thing you could do in any given situation. Wildly inappropriate behavior. Random violence. Shouting obscenities in church, screaming slurs on the bus. Grabbing the doctor with the stethoscope pressed to your chest and shoving your tongue down their throat. Picking up the knife on a dinner date and lunging across the table. Jumping from a bridge you happen to be crossing on your way to somewhere. Kebab skewers going into your eyes instead of the grilled lamb and green peppers. Nothing you would ever *want* to do. Which is why it comes: precisely because you don't want to do it, for an instant, you can think of nothing else.

Maybe that's what happens to us, she muses, her steady footfalls matching the rhythm of the pulse in her ears. When we catch it. Maybe that part of us gets free for real and for good and takes over, and gets to finally do all those things.

Which means, when we catch it, it doesn't put anything in us that wasn't already there.

She's thinking about these things so she doesn't have to think about Ellis. She's perfectly cognizant of that.

Surely that's all it is.

But the crows scream, and it comes back to her like the thought about the window: the smashed body in front of her, the crushed head, the rock in her hands, and the single baleful eye. How it was so easy that she didn't even know she was doing it until it was already done. How for a fraction of a second, her head might have smashed through the glass as easily as the crow's skull smashed beneath her blows.

Fragment of a line from somewhere, absent context and sense, and yet it makes all the sense in the world.

Between the motion and the act falls the shadow.

What waits in that shadow?

Does it have eyes?

Is it looking?

25

It's not yet dusk by the time she reaches home, the sun hasn't even touched the distant line of oaks across the lake, but the world feels darker. Riley pauses on the bank and gazes out at the sullen red circle sinking toward that green rim, and notes how the water is so still that the reflection is nearly unbroken, a flawless mirror image if one only glanced.

This was out of her way. Instead of following the path straight up to the house, she turned and made her way down the slight slope to the water's edge, and here she stands, without any real notion of why.

She keeps doing things without knowing why. She feels troubled, albeit at an odd remove, like observing an emotion without actually feeling it. Observing the reflection of the sun rather than the sun itself.

Of course, if you look directly at the sun, it can blind you.

This is where she threw her cell phone into the water. Perhaps not the exact spot, but close enough. Before, she thought of it being entombed in mud and discovered some unquantifiable length of time in the future by an archeologist, should humanity survive so long as to produce them that far from the present. Now she wonders if it's even here anymore or if some current might have carried it away.

It's dead. No matter how tough it is, it must be dead. It's been in the water for days. It's literally impossible for it to be anything more than a useless lump of plastic and circuitry. And all the same she's filled with the urge, not quite the image, to leap into the lake and dive, furiously scour the mud as the light bleeds out of the world and not stop until she finds it. Recovers it somehow. Her last connection. She concluded that without it she was drifting free in a way she never had been before, but she hadn't understood the full terror of what that might mean—drifting away from *herself*, from what's *real*, from what makes *sense*.

Even if it wasn't dead, do you think a fucking cell phone could fix what's wrong here? What's broken?

Don't you have a friend you could ask for help? Don't you have a friend you could hold on to? Isn't Ellis all you have left?

She hugs herself and squeezes her eyes shut. After a while, she turns her back on the sun—now grazing the oaks—and climbs the slope to the house.

Thinking, as she does, not of a boat untied from its dock and drifting away into the water but instead of a boat anchored far out, far enough to see nothing but water and sky, and the chain that binds it to the anchor snapping and the boat drifting, inexorably, horribly, toward the cruelly jagged rocks on the shore.

26

She's not dreaming. She's sure of that.

She is in bed, and she was trying to sleep. The power has cut out again, blinked off as she was sitting in the recliner and reading a book without really processing a single word and firmly not thinking of the sensation of Ellis's lips on her skin, and instead of digging into her store of candles—which is honestly dwindling—or pulling out the solar-powered lantern, she simply put the book down and went to bed.

She doesn't know how long ago that was. She turned over, turned again, again, was too hot, kicked the covers off, was freezing, and pulled them back up. She couldn't seem to get her heart rate down. She curled fetal, and sweat itched between her thighs and belly and under her breasts. Is she getting sick? It's been years since she was sick. It's been years since she was close enough to someone to catch anything.

Well.

She watches the crooked rectangle patch of moonlight sliding little by little across the floor. It is the only sign she has that time is indeed proceeding in a forward manner, and it is therefore bleakly comforting.

Until it touches a pair of feet.

The feet are bare and attached to a pair of legs. The legs are bare as well, to the knees, at which point they disappear under a fall of colorless cloth, and there the moonlight ends. Riley hasn't lifted her gaze beyond the reach of the light. She doesn't seem able to move at all.

She's not dreaming. She really is sure. But it occurs to her that this might be sleep paralysis, in which case she can't trust anything she sees. It's been a very long time since it happened to her, but it's not the sort of thing you forget. The inability to make her limbs respond. The awful pressure on her chest. One time, a rhythmic crashing sound that seemed to be coming from something right beside her head, unseen, just beyond her immobile field of vision.

Never any figures, though, shadowy and demonic or otherwise. Never any legs and feet.

Those feet could be anyone's and everyone's. Old friends from school whose faces she barely recalls. Teachers. Strangers. The elderly man who was her neighbor before he leaped from his window and smashed his head open on the street. Everyone she ever saw die that way, senseless and bloody, that howling madness from deep within the brain ascendant and finally triumphant.

Her grandparents. Although she wasn't here for that. It's not as though she hasn't imagined it plenty of times, vividly and very much against her will.

Ellis.

No. It isn't any of those people. She knows those feet. Her certainty is only confirmed when the owner takes a step forward—or the light shifts on its own, the moon jerking abruptly in the sky like a spotlight swinging across a stage—and the patch of light touches hips, torso, shoulders, and face.

Face streaked with gore, punctuated by raw empty eye sockets clotted with old blood.

Her mother stands motionless, looking at her with those holes where her eyes once rested. Riley doesn't move either—doesn't breathe, can't breathe, can't ask her mother what she wants, what she's doing here, can't scream and scream.

Her mother's hands are hanging at her sides, but one isn't loose. It's closed around something, and now Riley sees that blood is dripping from between her fingers and hitting the floor in a soft, rhythmic *pat-pat*.

That hand rises. Turns palm up and opens. And her mother's eyes are there, optic nerves trailing like little tails, and they're staring at her, staring into her, piercing the space between them and ripping through her sclera and pupil and retina and stabbing into her brain.

Look away look away lookawaylookawayLOOKAWAY

"You didn't take these with you when you left," her mother says. Her tone is gently chiding, as though Riley has neglected to do some promised chore or come home past curfew. "You should have, you went to so much trouble to get them."

No. That's wrong. That's not fair. *You did it, Mom. You did it to yourself.*

"Oh, sweetheart." The smile that peels her mother's lips back from her teeth is ghastly. "Did you forget? You did, didn't you?" She takes a step toward the bed, slow and jerky, still proffering her eyes. But it hits Riley then that her mother can still see through them, that she's using them to look at Riley right now.

With everything that entails.

"Maybe you just can't hear," her mother says softly, "with that voice so loud in your head."

That crashing sound beside her ear, sudden and deafening, only it's inside her, right in the center of her skull, and it's not a crash, not an impact at all; it's a howl, a scream, shrill and mad, the world-shredding shriek of an immense crow. Yet somehow her mother is audible over the din, quite clear, and she reaches the bed and bends over Riley, like she's preparing a good-night kiss for her daughter before she tucks her in.

"Here," she murmurs. "Take them." And with a single thrust, she jams them into Riley's eye sockets.

27

Light.

Sunlight, harsh, striking her in the face. She blinks and winces, turns her head into the pillow, and squeezes her eyes shut. Her first muzzy thought is that she's hungover, her head pounding with the brightness. But she didn't drink last night. She couldn't have; there's no alcohol in the house. Her eyes feel huge, swollen, the lids crusted and gritty.

Her eyes.

With a violent twitch, she's sitting upright, her hands flying to her face and feeling that grit, wiping it onto her fingers, and when she examines them, she's sure that she'll see flakes of dried blood.

Nothing but a few yellowish grains.

She exhales and drops her hands to her sides. Stupid. She's had a bizarre few days, she's struggling to come to grips with it, and she had a nightmare. That's all. Understandable. Predictable, even.

Groaning, she swings her legs over the side of the bed, maneuvers herself upright, half staggers into the bathroom, and splashes handfuls of cold water on her face. It feels better, she feels more present and her eyes less swollen, but as she rubs her face dry and raises her head to the blank place on the wall where the mirror used to be—

Riley's eyes are brown, like her father's. But her mother's are blue.

Were blue.

If that mirror were here now, and she could look into it, what color would her eyes be?

You could always go ask Ellis. Ask Ellis to look and see. You might even get an answer before you die.

She shakes her head, shoves herself away from the sink and strides back into the bedroom. She very purposefully avoids looking at the floor as she passes the bed. There's no need to do that. She already knows she won't see anything.

28

But there is Ellis.

Ellis comes back to her thoughts. Won't leave them. She eats a breakfast she doesn't taste, wanders around the house—avoiding the bloodstains in the hall just as she did the spot on the bedroom floor where there were of course no stains at all. Just as she didn't taste her food, she wanders without seeing much of anything. It feels to her that no time is passing at all, that she woke up into a single frozen moment and has been unable to leave it.

Yet this isn't the first time someone's made her feel that way. In the kitchen, she pauses and shuts her eyes, fists clenched. The memory comes, rising from the depths of her all covered in barnacles and seaweed like a ghost ship surfacing after countless submerged centuries. She doesn't want to think of this now. She put it away. She hadn't wanted to think of it at all, after it happened.

That was the whole fucking point.

When she was fifteen, she went on a date. The boy was older than she was by a good three years, which was flattering and exciting. They went to a movie—although some aspects of the night are piercingly clear to her now, she can't for the life of her recall what the movie itself was—and then to a diner, and this boy behaved himself perfectly well. But he offered to drive her home, and instead of doing that, he drove them to a back road not far from the high school football field, and beneath the dense shadows of old maples, he tried to get his hands under her shirt. And of course when she said no, she didn't want to do that, he got more aggressive. Much more. Pinned her down in the seat and shoved her legs apart with his knee and started pushing up her skirt.

Tale as old as fucking time.

She panicked. She recognized that later, knew it for what it was. Rage, certainly, but over the rage was utter blinding terror, which—instead of paralyzing her—shocked her muscles into frantic motion, and without ever meaning to, without ever having come to the decision to do so, she fought him. She fought him with her nails and with her teeth, half bit his lower lip off, jammed her knee clumsily into his balls, scored his cheek, and packed blood and flesh under her purple-lacquered fingernails.

She made it out of the car and ran. She ran all the way to the high school and kept on running the five blocks to home. Only once she was inside did she realize how badly her clothes were torn and disarrayed, the blood on her face and hands, the bruises on her wrists and one thigh.

Her father was working the late shift. Her mother had wanted to call the police. Still buzzing and numb with adrenaline fallout, Riley had refused. She didn't want to talk to cops. She didn't want to open that door and walk through. She wanted to shower and go to bed. She wanted to not think about it anymore.

So for about a week—a week she can barely remember even now in the midst of this vivid recall—she didn't think about anything. She drifted, aimless, with no plan or goal.

It's ridiculous, the association between that time and this. It's her brain lunging wildly for any point of reference that might help her make sense of things. What Ellis did wasn't an assault. Ellis hardly did anything at all.

But it's still a door she doesn't want to walk through. It's still a line of thought she doesn't want to follow. Because it won't stay merely a thought. It won't stay in her head. It'll make other things happen. She's as sure of that as she is of anything.

So she's drifting.

It's not the only door you're not walking through.

She sways slightly, hands braced on the counter, eyes closed against the sun—a sun which she'd swear hasn't moved. The house spins around her. A house of endless dark hallways lined with closed doors behind which wait things unspeakable. Neatly snipped computer cables. The impression of a foot in soil. The indistinct movement of shadows through glass. Bloodstains on the floor. Her own fucking eyes.

Jesus Christ, get a grip. *On what?* On anything at all.

The thing about being alone for so long, she thinks, is that little by little, all the edges smooth out and there's nothing left to dig your fingers into.

29

Okay. Okay, so she'll try to find a crack or cranny to dig her fingers into. Running her hands over everything, slowly and carefully and above all methodically. She doesn't have any reason to rush. She's safe in this house.

Are you?

Line by line, item by item. She sits on the floor beside the old bloodstains, the sun spilling generously over them, tracing the smears and spatters on the wood with a fingertip. Somehow they're grounding, a material thing to focus on, real and constant. Been here since she arrived, like some kind of final message, like a note left on a kitchen counter.

The equilibrium of everything has shifted; some new variable has knocked it all off-kilter. What new variable is there? Only one. What do these unsettling events most feel like?

Someone is fucking with her.

What possible reason would Ellis have to fuck with her? How would said fuckery integrate with how Ellis has behaved toward her so far? Ellis has been polite. Respectful. Hospitable. Friendly, which must be an extremely unusual thing to be these days.

Friendly. Close. Very close. Close enough to touch, which is close enough to slip.

Reckless. Dangerous.

Riley draws her knees up and hugs them, rocks back against the wall. She settles there for a moment and then goes on rocking, chewing at her lower lip, staring at the blood. There must have been so much of it. It must have jetted from the opened veins with considerable force, at least until the pressure subsided. The constant pressure that pushes the blood endlessly through us is delicately balanced. Disrupted in that way, it explodes everywhere. Makes such a mess. And works against us; it's that very pressure that causes us to bleed out in minutes.

Does Ellis want to infect her?

She gapes at the question. Its very premise is incomprehensible. Everyone used the language of disease and contagion from the beginning because there was no other way to describe what it does, but no one was ever able to prove it was a virus. No one was ever able to explain it at all. Viruses exist to propagate themselves; the destruction of the host is, if anything, an undesirable side effect of that process. Creatures infected with rabies attack and bite to spread the virus; there is no other practical reason for the violence. This violence . . . It hasn't ever seemed like that. It's not an attempt on the part of the contagion to spread.

It is, apparently, merely what happens when someone's mind destroys itself.

Why would Ellis want to infect her? Nothing about that question makes any fucking sense. If Ellis wanted to infect her, it would be suicidal, and in any case, Ellis could have already done it in a hundred different ways at a hundred different points. She did see reports of it happening: when people who hadn't yet been infected lost their minds in a far more conventional manner and intentionally did it to both themselves and others. But in those cases, it was wild and disorganized. It wasn't slow and manipulative.

It wasn't seduction.

Unless, again, it's changed. Mutated, somehow, and now all the rules are different.

And how would you know?

Why would Ellis be fucking with her? Why would Ellis be trying to infect her, suicide directly into her eyes? Maybe Ellis is insane, mad in a concealed and lurking way that can make itself seem normal for a time but mad nevertheless. Insanity isn't rare. Awful lot of it's been going around the last few years.

Maybe Ellis is already infected.

And it just doesn't kill you fast anymore. Maybe it lies mostly dormant in your brain, takes its time to eat through you. Maybe it only rises to the surface and manifests itself days or weeks later. Even years. It could happen. Other things work that way. Maybe it's not even a new mutation, if whatever this is can mutate at all. Maybe it's been like this for a while and it's just that no one ever figured it out. Maybe it's been like this since the beginning. Some of us come apart right away, but for some of us, it takes a long, long time.

Maybe, when we finally do go to pieces, we still like to have a little company in the midst of it. Maybe we just don't want to dissolve into that seething internal chaos alone.

Alone.

Riley turns her head toward the sun, presses her cheek against the top of her knees, and rocks a little faster. Through her mostly closed lids, the world is a brilliant red.

It would be better if she didn't see Ellis again. It would be better if she remained alone. Safer. There's too much she doesn't know, can't know anymore. Don't know, can't trust.

What she does know is how to be alone. She's been doing it for long enough.

It may not be up to you.

The neatly severed cables. In the house. Not just outside in the yard, in the flower bed, but in the fucking house.

No. Riley did that herself. She must have. Did it and forgot, or did it in her sleep, or—

So now you're the crazy one?

Softly, she moans, lowers her knees, and grips the sides of her head and pulls at her hair until her eyes water. She can't do this. It's not fair. This is what she came out here to get away from. Get away from people, simplify everything, be *safe*—as much as *safe* is possible anymore. It's too easy, with people, to find yourself doing things you can't take back. It's too easy to fuck up and discover that you've done something that undoes everything forever. People get inside you and they *change* you, and then the old you is gone forever, and you have to live with the new you, whom you may or may not even recognize.

Who may do terrible things. Terrible, unforgivable things.

But it felt good, she thinks, to be that close. Even now she's thinking about it, turning her face back to the warmth of the sun, and the hair on her arms and the back of her neck is rising, as if reaching for something.

She shouldn't.

Maybe that's why you want to.

30

Once again, she wanders the house. She spends the rest of the day doing it. She eventually emerges from the house itself and circles the yard, prowling over every inch, scrutinizing, and not quite telling herself what she's looking at, looking for. There is no one thing. Taking inventory, perhaps. Impressing as vividly as possible onto her memory how everything looks and is arranged—the configuration of objects, the patchy distribution of dust, the exact placement of every leaf and every blade of grass. She should know it all by heart and at a glance, but now she's second-guessing. Is it the way it's always been? Has something else changed? Are those depressions her footprints? Were they there five minutes ago? Standing very still and listening, hearing nothing but the wind in the trees. Feeling, distinctly, the sensation of being watched.

She lifts her gaze to those whispering trees and sees row upon row of cold black eyes above sharp black beaks, each one drilling into her.

She hastily turns away. Everything becomes sort of blurry for a while, and when she can focus again, she's eating food that she doesn't taste, sitting at the kitchen table under lighting—the power is on tonight—that seems harsher and more abrasive than it should be. She isn't even entirely certain what she's prepared; something from a box, something that doesn't take long and requires only salt and water. There's so much that she can't cook anymore, so much she can't get the ingredients for—or the ingredients are far too expensive and getting worse all the time.

And then she realizes, on the way up to bed, that without a computer or a phone, it's going to be next to impossible to get any more of almost anything. Unless she risks going into town. If the car will even start, which she isn't confident about.

Or unless she goes to Ellis.

Ellis. In bed, watching the shadows warp and weave on the ceiling, she thinks about Ellis and about everything she's attaching to Ellis, the different ways to categorize this new variable. The looming threat, the potential of obscure malevolence, the possibility of literal insanity, the sheer unpredictability of what can't ever be completely known, and the danger that lurks within that.

The warm breath on the back of her neck, the shell of her ear, and the hands that aren't her own. The body that isn't her own. The intention. These things are lethal weapons, she knows. These things can kill. But wasn't that always true? You go to bed with someone. You sleep. Couldn't they always have killed you, even before this strained new world? Weren't you always defenseless beside them? Isn't that part of why we do it, whether or not we want to admit it to ourselves?

She thinks in old movie reel flickers of the elderly couple sleeping peacefully and conventionally side by side, and then someone bound and blindfolded, gasping and pressing eagerly against leather, breath held in the clenched fist of the heart as the blade of a knife slides down their naked ribs.

Wasn't this edge always there?

Or I'm just crazy, she muses, noting her own hands wandering over her belly, slipping up under her tank top, and nosing under the waistband of her underwear. *Or it's just me, I'm out of my mind, I'm a freak, and normal uninfected people never think this way.* About unseen hands doing exactly what hers are doing now and a body lying along her back, warm and solid as a dream. Moving slightly, rolling against hers just so, her ass so nearly in the cradle of unseen hips as one set of rough fingers trace the underside of her breast and the other explores the edges of the thatch of curls between her thighs. We can do it like this, can't we, mouth the lips at the nape of her neck, the silent flicker of a tongue. It's safe like this. Just watch the shadows.

Safe.

But they're so close, aren't they? Twin knives pressed against the back of her skull, twin muzzles of two loaded and cocked guns, twin bullets ready to pierce her retinas and shred her brain. Her teeth shut on her lower lip as her pinched nipple sends sparkles along her nerves and those curious fingers graze the hood of her clit, press down, and a hard gust of wind like a sigh stirs the shadows into a colorless blur. They're so close. It's never safe to be close like this. You're always dancing along the edge of a blade. But it's so lovely when it shines.

She moans and rolls farther onto her back, kicking at the sheet, her legs falling open. It feels so good. She doesn't know when she last felt so good, doesn't know when it last occurred to her that she could. Like something long-closed in her has been cracked open, a lock picked, a door creaking open, something sliding through the crack—fingers, like sliding easy and slick into her and curving slightly upward, beckoning.

Come here.

Warm, solid body levering over hers and braced above her, spreading her legs wider, and she almost cries out, because this isn't safe at all, this was never safe, but it's so *good*, thick fingers pumping faster into her cunt and a mouth so tantalizingly close to hers. Face close. Eyes close. Closed or open? Hers are closed. Not watching the shadows, not watching anything; only the seething dark behind her lids. Only what she'd maybe see if she had no eyes at all, if she cut them out and held them in her hands, felt that softness and that slick.

She could open her eyes. She does have them, and she could use them. A lurching moan escapes her as she thinks of it. What it would be like. She's close and she's *close*, racing along the edge, and she could just—

Look.

Maybe it's like this when it gets into you, a strangely remote part of her muses as she snaps her hips up, rigid, teeth bared against her shout. Maybe it's not bad after all. Maybe it feels good, like everything letting go. Maybe it feels like coming.

She lies there half tangled in the sheet, breathing hard, wet fingers curled at her side and drying cool and sticky. Reflexively, she lifts them to her mouth and sucks at them. Tastes familiar salt and almost sweet.

And metallic tang? Iron?

Something thumps in the hall.

She jerks herself upright, clutching at the sheet, her eyes wide, listening so hard the air rings.

Nothing. She imagined it. She slipped off the edge for a moment, and she just imagined it. There's nothing there.

She doesn't move. Keeps listening, barely daring to breathe.

There's something about that silence that she doesn't like. They're of a completely different quality, an empty silence and a silence that is most definitely occupied.

Keeping her eyes locked on the bedroom door—narrow rectangle of deeper darkness in the middle of a sea of unsteady shadows—she gropes at the bedside table. For a few seconds, she isn't sure what she's even searching for; then her fingertips touch the smooth, cool handle and she knows what it is. She doesn't recall bringing the knife to bed, but she knows.

The flash of it comes to her, a single frame cut from that inner filmstrip: her lying on the bed, legs wide, frantically fucking herself with it, blood pooling under her and turning the sheets black, her head thrown back and her mouth open and twisted in silent, wild laughter.

She shudders and almost drops the knife. *Stop it. Stop. That's not you.*

It's not in you.

Her bare feet hit the cool floor, and she's standing. Gripping the knife's handle like a railing as she moves toward the door, and now that the hideous image has faded, it's reassuring. She's not vulnerable. She can protect herself. She can fight back. Against—

She stops in the doorway, brandishing the knife with one hand, and with the other she feels the wall by the door for the light switch. Flicks it, it clicks softly, and the bedroom is bathed in sudden, searing light that spills into the hall, and in an instant, she sees it: a tall, powerful human figure standing at the opposite end of the hallway by the head of the stairs, head cocked, staring at her.

She slaps her hand over the top half of her face as a soft cry rips out of her, panic jittering her nerves. *Did you see them. Did you see their eyes. Oh God, did you* see.

Nothing. Again, nothing. The nothing is starting to be as fundamentally frightening to her as Something might be.

Cautiously, she lowers her hand and blinks into the dimness. Sees not a person standing there but instead her own silhouette cast by the bedroom light, stretching down the short length of the hall to the other wall. On which—she can't immediately tell if it's scrawled or gouged into the plaster—is one word, over and over, and as her gaze slides away and over the other walls, there it is again, large and small and jumbled, spread, a meandering senseless labyrinth of words etched in the clumsy all-caps chicken scratch of an insane kindergartner.

LOOK LOOK LOOK LOOK LOOK LOOK LOOK LOOK LOOK LOOK

She takes a step forward. Another. Reaches up with her free hand and traces one of the words, big and diagonal beside the bathroom doorframe. The lines jagged and tactile; carved.

With an effort, she works saliva into her dry mouth and swallows. She has to get hold of herself. She has to be sharp. She's not safe. Someone could be here. Whoever did this could still be in the house.

Sure. Sure, they could. They could be right here, right this second.

"I didn't do this," she whispers. "I didn't fucking do this."

It would have taken time to do it, though, if someone else did. There's a lot of it, not quite floor to ceiling but covering a good bit. She wasn't in bed for that long. It would have taken time, and it also would have been noisy. She would have heard it. She wasn't even asleep.

A bit distracted, though, weren't you?

She moves farther into the hall, cuts on the light. The words don't disappear under more direct illumination; she's weirdly dismayed to discover that part of her hoped they might. She steps into the bathroom, pulls in a breath, and shoves aside the shower curtain with the flat of the knife. Nothing but the tub, badly in need of the scrubbing that she never seems to find the motivation to do.

The other bedroom, which is full of unlabeled boxes and devoid of anyone but her. The closet; only old clothes and the fabric-decay smell of an ancient thrift store.

Down the stairs. The words stop at the landing. Below is the darkened downstairs hall. She hears nothing but the crickets outside and the hiss of the wind.

She's feeling decreasingly scared and increasingly stupid as she searches the rest of the house room by room and finds no one, nothing, not even more scratches in the walls. In the end, she's standing in the kitchen, still holding the knife, the house a blaze of light in a way she can't recall it being since she moved in. Even the basement; the sullen yellowish glow of a naked bulb shines up from the open door. No one is here. No one but her.

Very slowly, she pulls a chair out from the kitchen

table and sinks into it, sets the knife down in front of her, and looks at it. Studies it, examines the point and the edge.

Is that old soap residue stuck in a tiny notch under the tip? Or is it plaster?

It could be any number of things. It doesn't mean anything. She could make herself crazy chasing her own mind in circles like this. She could drive herself insane trying to untangle it all, and she can't afford that right now. She exhales and sits back, gazes blankly up at the ceiling.

Something is very wrong. She's not safe. And she's all alone.

After a while, the lights go out.

She wakes up still in the kitchen chair, her head pillowed on her arms and a small puddle of drool on the table-top. Her back is killing her; her neck is worse. She pushes herself upright and rubs at her eyes in the thin morning light, her face, dry-washing, struggling free of sleep that feels more like being drugged. Something happened last night, she does remember that. Something that explains why she's down here, and why there's a knife on the table in front of her, and why she suddenly and violently doesn't want to go upstairs.

She does, though. And has to sit down in the hall, the knife in her lap and her spine pressed uncomfortably against the wooden banister, staring at the words carved into the walls.

She can't go on like this. This absolutely cannot continue.

What in the blue fuck do you expect to be able to do about it? Call a shrink?

She can't call anyone. So that really leaves only one other option.

Twenty minutes later, she's showered and dressed and striding down her driveway toward the road.

With another, smaller knife neatly tucked into her sock.

31

Riley pauses for a while at the gate, distantly grateful that the house isn't visible from the road. It gives her time to work herself up to this. To conjure the notion of what she might do and what she might have no choice about doing.

But as before, there are certain things she's not conjuring. Can't. Won't. The knife was bad enough. That it's here is bad enough. She not only allowed but forced herself to wonder, in the early days: Could she go that far, if she had to? Could she do that to someone?

Never came down on any answer she was confident of.

She reaches into her pocket and pulls out her blinders, and with her gaze locked on the ground in front of her, she starts toward Ellis's house.

Her soft knock isn't immediately answered. She listens; no sound from inside. She hesitates, adjusts the blinders over her eyes, knocks again a bit louder.

Still nothing.

It's a reprieve, she thinks wildly. She put in the effort; she's performed what rationality requires of her and she can go home now. Nothing to be done if Ellis simply isn't here. She doesn't have to deal with this today—and maybe she doesn't have to deal with it at all. Maybe Ellis decided that Riley was too much weird trouble as a neighbor and simply left.

Or got bored with her.

Got bored with trying to nudge you over the edge.

"Honestly wasn't sure I'd see you again."

She spins around, nearly ducks down to grope for the knife. It hits her, seconds after: if she hadn't had her blinders on, that might have been it. The whole business might have been moot.

Unless the rules changed and you just don't know about it yet.

Or unless it was too late for you a long time ago, and you've just been wrong for all these years about what the rules even are.

She blinks at the dark, indistinct lines that comprise her vision behind the thick glass. All vague shapes, interpretable only because she already knows what they are. The jagged black of the trees, the anemic sliver of light that is the sunny sky. A humanoid shape standing against the slightly lighter background that is the gravel; difficult to say with any certainty how far away. Standing between her and the way to the road.

Too late. She can't back out now. She's committed.

She shrugs, trying to come across casual. "I just needed some time to think."

Not wholly untrue, albeit not the whole truth.

"Yeah. I guess I did, too. I'm sorry," Ellis adds, and the tone is almost impossible to decipher. Guarded, perhaps more than anything. "I'm sorry if I . . . made you uncomfortable before. It wasn't my intention."

"What *did* you intend?"

Her own question startles her in its directness.

"I don't know," Ellis says quietly. "I don't think I intended anything much. It wasn't like that. It just happened."

Riley cocks her head, her eyes narrowed as if that might help her perceive with any clarity in a world of unclear shadows. "What would you call it, what happened?"

In the world Before, it would probably be reasonable for Ellis to tell her to fuck off if an interrogation is all this is going to be. But that was Before, and instead, Ellis—going by body language—appears to be giving the question some thought.

And anyway, they're friends. Aren't they? Isn't that the word for what they are?

"I wanted to be closer to you," Ellis says finally. "What I wanted besides that, I'm not sure. But I know I wanted that. It's been a long time since I was close to anyone."

Riley exhales heavily, steps forward, sinks down on the porch steps. All of a sudden, her very skeleton feels heavy. And like this, it's easier to get to the knife.

Ellis comes closer, but stops short of sitting down beside her. Remains standing instead, leaning back against the railing and melting into the deeper shadow of the house.

"You said you were with someone," Riley says presently. "Before."

"I was."

"And you left them. But they didn't die."

"I did. And they didn't." Pause. "I told you I couldn't do it anymore. I get how maybe that sounds . . . evasive or something, but there really isn't a whole lot more to it than that. Everything changed and I just didn't know how to be with someone any longer. It wasn't only the danger, it was something else. Something deeper. It was like there was this . . . black *nothingness* opening up between us and getting wider every day, every hour, and pretty soon, I wouldn't be able to see them anymore across the divide."

Riley gnaws at a cuticle. That makes a kind of sense that lies beyond sense and entirely in the realm of feeling. "So you left."

"Ripped off the fucking Band-Aid." A touch of wryness. "Thing is, in some ways, it wasn't as hard for them as it was for me, the transition to not being able to make eye contact."

Riley drops her hands back onto her knees. "Why not? Were they blind?"

"Autistic. Eye contact was really unpleasant for them. Unsettling. So we were already kind of . . . used to that part, I guess. I don't know," Ellis continues, softer. "I don't know what exactly it was. I just couldn't be there anymore. And I felt like shit, leaving, but I didn't know what else to do. I didn't know what would happen if I stayed. If someone called me a coward for that, I wouldn't argue."

Riley says nothing. A sudden rustle in a nearby tree, a bird's scream. A crow?

"After that is when I ended up in the gated community I mentioned. Didn't buy a house or anything, just moved in. No one questioned it. A lot of houses are just vacant now. Sometimes it's an issue when bills don't get paid, and sometimes it's not. There's no logic to it. No one really cares." Ellis sighs, and it's soaked in a sort of exhaustion that seems to weigh down Riley's bones even more.

"Why are you telling me all this?" Riley asks, low.

"Because there's a lot I haven't told you. And I get the feeling you don't totally trust me, and this seems like . . . I don't know. Like maybe telling you more about me could help with that."

Again, Riley doesn't answer. Through the fabric of her sock, the edge of the blade is digging into her ankle, a sensation just short of a sting. The sting is in her eyes beneath her blinders, and she pulls in a shuddering breath, ducking her head. She's so fucking tired. She shouldn't have come here.

"I don't know either," she whispers, folds her hands, and presses them against her forehead. "I think I'm losing my goddamn mind."

"Why?" Terribly gentle. For some unfathomable reason, it almost makes her angry. "What's going on?"

"I don't *know*," she repeats tersely. The cables. The footprints. The figures in the dark. The words scratched into the walls. A litany of insanity she has no idea how to deliver. "I think someone is fucking with me."

"Fucking with—Why? Who would do that?" Then, immediately and flat with quiet realization: "You thought maybe I was."

"Are you?"

She despises how desperately miserable she sounds.

"No. No, I'm not. I swear I'm not. Riley." The light, hesitant weight of a hand on her shoulder, and poison surges up in her. The wounded animal urge to snap and bite. "I think you've been alone for too long."

Yes. No. She's been alone for too long. It was a mistake to ever stop being alone. Leaning closer to that comforting hand, turning her head and nuzzling her jaw against Ellis's wrist, plunging her hand into her sock and whipping out the knife and slicing through whatever flesh she can reach. Veins like cut cables. Shoving her head between her knees and screaming. Pulling off her blinders and stabbing her own treacherous eyes out. Her mother's empty, bloody sockets, glistening in the light from the street outside.

You've been alone for too long. This is exactly what someone fucking with her would say. To get closer. Which Ellis said. That's what Ellis intended. Closer.

"Can you tell me what's been happening?"

But Riley is already on her feet and stumbling blindly forward, nearly falling, catching herself against a tree and shaking her blinders off. Behind her, Ellis is saying something, voice rising in concern, but she's not allowing the words to penetrate. She can't believe them. She can't afford to. They're reassuring her toward disaster.

She doesn't know what the rules are.

"I can't see you anymore," she gasps, not turning. "Stay the fuck away from me."

The blinders slip from her fingers, and she hears the glass crunch between her foot and the gravel as she begins to run.

32

She guesses at the path rather than sees it, her breath hectic and pulsing in her lungs, and she pauses only long enough to listen over her panting, to try to detect any indication of pursuit. If Ellis is chasing her—

If Ellis is chasing her, that would be a very stupid thing to do.

Distantly, some practicalities are reasserting themselves. Ellis has a phone. As far as Riley is aware, a functioning car. Ellis was her last safe link to the outside. But Ellis is not safe. There's no way to be sure that Ellis is safe.

There's no way to be sure of anything.

She can't recall with any clarity when she left the house, but it seems to her that it's getting dark now, very dark, more rapidly than it should. Like a storm blowing in. She peers up at the sky; no clouds that she can see. But here under the trees, it's becoming difficult to make out the path, and the world is throbbing at the edges. She presses her fingers to her temples, pauses, and bends double.

Screams above her. A wild chorus of them, cutting through the air like knives. She looks up, breath snagging in her chest, and sees so many eyes in the trees staring down at her, eyes and black fluttering shapes, so many that the trees themselves might be made of them. One standing in the path directly in front of her—the largest crow she's ever seen, head cocked, gaze fixing her in place, and its eye is not the beady ink drop of a bird's but a human eye, massive in its head, sclera shocking white against the black feathers and the iris a brilliant and familiar blue.

Riley shrieks and rushes at it. The knife scrapes her ankle, but she doesn't reach for it—that would require more conscious intention than she has now; her hands are outstretched to grab the bird, no idea what she'll do when she gets hold of it, only anything to make it stop *looking* at her with those awful eyes.

It leaps into the air before she gets to it, and she stumbles and goes down hard, palms smacking painfully against the packed dirt and her knees burning with impact and friction. She whimpers and pushes herself up, examining her hands; beads of blood on her right from where she landed on the edge of a mostly buried rock. The knees of her jeans are ripped, the skin beneath red and raw.

She raises her head and sees nothing but the trees. Hears nothing but wind and distant birdsong.

You're in trouble, some stubbornly rational part of her murmurs. *Oh, girl, you're in so much trouble. You may not even know how much yet.*

She just has to get home. She'll get home, lock up the house as well as she can, and think. Figure it out from there, the way she always has. She's always been okay in the end. The world broke, and she was okay. She was alone, and she was okay. Lost her mother and she was okay. She'll merely make it work again, is all.

Wincing, she gets to her feet and limps onward. She doesn't look up again all the rest of the way. She makes it. Stands in the front hall and breathes in what she can believe for a few moments is safety. She's okay.

Five minutes after she locks the front door, there's a heavy knocking, and *okay* no longer has any meaning.

33

She doesn't open it. She stares at it, turning the knife back and forth in her hand. Not the one she took to Ellis's house; this is the big carving knife from the block, the one she had beside her bed, and the weight is comforting. Real.

A brief pause, and silence. Then another round of knocking, this time with a more insistent air. Not quite pounding.

She told Ellis to stay away. So far, Ellis has been very willing to give her space. But mightn't that have changed now, if Ellis perceives that the quarry is slipping away?

Or just doesn't want to give up on her?

She could look out the peephole, verify for certain who it is—and if not Ellis, then who? But that might go very wrong. She might encounter uncovered eyes. That might be what she's *supposed* to encounter. This might be in every respect a trap. One look out and then she's alone in here and tumbling into the abyss, slitting her own throat with the weapon she got to defend herself.

The knocking has stopped. For a long moment, there's nothing further. She allows herself to hope that whoever it is might have gone away.

She knows that's not the case.

"Hello?"

Not Ellis's voice. Deeper. Rougher. Mocking lilt in it, Riley thinks—*helloooooo*—and in a sickening rush, she's positive. It's marvelous how abruptly and totally the doubts melt away. It wasn't Ellis after all—or not Ellis alone. The figure standing in her yard. The figure standing in her hall. Sensing she's at a breaking point and finally emerging from the shadows to finish the job.

Either she takes control now, or she won't be able to at all anymore.

The speaker is saying something else, but she doesn't hear it over the roaring in her head and the bizarrely loud click of the latch as she yanks the door open. She can't think now. She doesn't have time to think. She likely has a few seconds at most in which to act. She perceives a man of medium height and stocky build, very pale, and sees his mouth pulled into a mocking sneer to match his tone, and with one hand, she seizes him by the shirt as she holds the knife to his neck and hauls him inside.

He doesn't resist. Perhaps he's too surprised. Didn't expect her to fight back, maybe. Grim satisfaction as she shifts her grip to his hair and jerks his head back, slams it as hard as she can against the wall. She hears something crunch and he drops bonelessly to the floor, leaves a smear of blood behind.

More blood. On the wall, on the floor. Leaving a long, ugly smear as she seizes his ankles and starts to drag him toward the kitchen.

34

The first thing she does when she gets him there is blindfold him.

In the process, she identifies the source of the blood; his nose is almost certainly broken, his lower lip split. The sorts of injuries that aren't fatal but bleed horribly. He's unconscious, not dead, but he's deadweight all the same as she maneuvers him—panting and straining—into a kitchen chair. She doesn't have rope easily on hand, doesn't want to leave him long enough to search for it, but torn strips of dishcloths and her grandmother's good linen napkins will probably be adequate. Especially since she doesn't anticipate that she'll need to hold him for long.

Could she really kill someone? If she had to, she believes she could. She realizes that she's always believed that. Some part of her has always known.

Once he's secured, she rocks back on her heels and studies him, idly turning the point of the knife against the linoleum. Whatever darkness was gathering in the forest has eased, and the sunlight is that of a warm and bright midafternoon.

He's approaching middle age, by her judgment, and his black hair is receding. Under the blood crusting his mouth and chin and jaw, he badly needs a shave, but that sort of personal hygiene was already something being generally abandoned by the time Riley withdrew from the world. His clothes—jeans, plaid flannel shirt, hiking boots—are worn, but beneath the wear, the make is obviously decent. She looks for a while at his boots, at the size, wishing she had a more vivid memory of the print in the flower bed. She should have measured it at the time. She wasn't thinking.

Nothing about him stands out. Nothing is obviously sinister. He just looks like a guy. Any one of a hundred million random guys.

But she knows she wasn't mistaking his tone and his expression.

Conspiring with Ellis? It hits her that Ellis was pointedly vague about the house, about coming into possession of it. His house, maybe? Imagining him hiding upstairs as she and Ellis talked in the living room, listening, or slipping out to her own house with a pair of clippers in his hand and that same sneer twisting his face. Why, though? Why would he? Why would the pair of them do that to her?

Unless they're already crazy. Infected or simply driven crazy by the world being the way it is; in practical terms it doesn't much matter, if the rules have changed and it doesn't always kill you right away, or people were wrong about the rules the whole time. And how would she know? How could she ever know for certain?

She'll wait until he wakes up, and she'll make him tell her. She'll make him say it.

Then she'll know.

35

"Who are you?"

He doesn't answer. He groans and pulls weakly at the binds. About ten minutes ago—by her reckoning—he began to stir, and it's borderline infuriating how slow he's been to return fully to consciousness, to the point where she's begun to suspect that he's faking it simply to frustrate her, to push her closer to whatever edge he's been driving her toward.

She leans forward in her own chair and presses the edge of the knife against his cheek, and he freezes. Aha. She smiles grimly; there's the alertness. He only needed the proper incentive. Maybe he's crazy, but that doesn't mean he doesn't fear pain, doesn't want to avoid injury.

She repeats the question very slowly, each word punctuated by more pressure on the knife. "Who. Are. You."

His lips curl, his arms stretching as he leans forward to match her. "I'm sure you'd love to know that." Pause. His smile fades. "I'm no one. It doesn't matter. Nothing matters."

"This matters." Dig of the knife into his jaw. She can feel that it wouldn't take much more pressure to break the skin. She honed the blade while she was waiting for him to wake up. "What I *want* matters right now, or it should matter to you."

"You want to know who I am? Take this blindfold off." He juts his chin tauntingly forward. "I promise, a lot of things will get a whole lot clearer for you."

Riley scoffs. "Seriously? You can't imagine I'm that stupid. Or that far gone. I know what you've been trying to do."

"Which is?"

"You've been trying to make me crazy," she says, hard and flat. "I don't know why, but I know that much. You've been fucking with me. Were you doing it alone, or were you working with Ellis?"

"Ellis?" He cocks his head, appears to be puzzled. Feigning puzzlement. "Oh, right. Yeah. Your neighbor. Maybe more than neighbor, mmm? *Friend?*" He bares his teeth, flash of yellowish white beneath the blindfold. "You been getting lonely, *Riley?*"

"Tell me. Now." She presses the point of the blade into the softer stubbled flesh under his chin. "Were you working with Ellis, or were you doing it alone?"

The man stiffens slightly, but allows no other indication that the threat of the knife is unsettling him. "Again, does it matter?" He grimaces. "How about a question for a question? Ellis shows up, all this weird shit starts happening, so did you suck at math in school, Riley? Can you stop shitting yourself long enough to do some basic addition?"

Spike of cold down her spine. It's one thing to suspect. Confirmation is something else entirely. You're never really ready for it.

"Why? Why the *fuck* are you doing this to me?"

"Take the blindfold off," the man murmurs. "Take it off and I'll show you why."

Riley withdraws the knife, looks at him for a long moment. He may not be precisely *forthcoming*, but he's clearly willing to say at least some things if it amuses him to do so. He's already given her some crucial information.

But again, likely it's mostly because it amused him to give it to her.

She looks down at the knife. It's intimidating, to be sure, but he can't see it. She's not a surgeon; she doesn't know where to cut to effectively hurt him, to maximize pain and minimize blood flow. It would be far too easy, with a tool like this, to accidentally bleed him into unconsciousness, or worse.

It's stunning, how coldly she's thinking this way. How she's capable of it. She didn't know; now she does. She has that much brutality in her, not merely to kill someone but to hurt them with a great deal more deliberation and care. Or she hasn't done it yet, but not because the prospect of doing so is too repellent.

She's on her own here, no cops to call, no one's brutality to depend on but her own, and she needs to know some things. This man is a monster. He's been tormenting her. Really, it's only what he deserves.

She gets up and moves over to the counter, to the knife block, and pulls out the shears.

He won't be able to see them. But if this is about math, she suspects he'll be able to work the equations when he feels it.

She goes back to him. Shears in hand, she crouches in front of him and doesn't take her eyes off his face as she grips his right hand where it rests on the arm of the chair, opens the blades, slides his forefinger between them. He gasps, goes rigid, and she's faintly appalled at her own smile.

"Tell me," she says slowly, "why you're doing this to me."

"Maybe I'm not doing anything."

"Bullshit. You've been watching me. You fucked up my computer, cut me off. So I'd get closer to Ellis, right? So I'd get dependent? The writing all over my walls. Why?"

Silence. Suddenly and violently, she does want to pull off the blindfold, see his eyes. It's impossible to know what he's thinking like this. If she could see his eyes, maybe he wouldn't have to tell her anything.

Like he said.

"Why are you trying to make me crazy?" she breathes.

Nothing.

Could you do it? If you had to? The shears tremble in her hand, unnaturally heavy, and she sees the crow, its smashed body and its single accusing eye piercing her, feels the weight of the rock. She could. She did. She has.

She doesn't know exactly what she expected, but she does know enough to realize that the way it looks in movies is never how it is in real life. In movies, this kind of thing always happens fast, and there may be a lot of screaming but for the most part, the gore is always minimal. So she's not altogether surprised when she closes the shears and the flesh parts under the blades, bright red welling up and flowing fast and heavy from the cut, but the blades stop when they meet bone and don't immediately proceed. He is screaming, shrieking loud enough to hurt her ears, and thrashing against the binds, his hand pulling frantically, and the movement makes the cut wider and messier, and the blood is making it difficult to see what she's doing.

Hold still, she wants to say. *You're making it worse. You're making it take longer.* And the absurdity of that—she *wants* to make it bad for him, doesn't she?—rolls hysterical laughter out of her as she jams her whole palm against the top of the shears and presses as hard as she can.

The resistance ends in an audible chopping crunch, and the bloody shears slip out of her grip and clatter onto the floor. His finger follows them. She stares at it. It's incongruous. It doesn't belong there on the floor in a pool of red, this piece of a living human being. It's not neat, the cut; the edges of the flesh are ragged, and the bits of pale bone she can see are broken and splintered.

She returns her gaze to him. He's slumped, sobbing, and he's bleeding quite a lot. Maybe too much. Maybe this wasn't such a good idea after all.

Cursing, she pushes to her feet and fetches another dish towel, stuffing it against the wound.

"Why are you trying to make me crazy?" Her voice is shaking, and she doesn't like that. Hopefully, he's too distracted to notice. "Tell me or you lose another one."

"I don't fucking need to make you crazy," he gasps. "Look at what you just *did,* for Christ's sake."

"That wasn't crazy. You *made* me, you wouldn't tell me what I want to know." But her focus keeps returning to the towel pressed against his hand, floral pink and green rapidly soaking with crimson. She did that. He made her, but she did it.

Made her.

Aren't you playing right into his hands?

"You're lying to yourself, you stupid bitch." The words come in rough, stuttering spurts between his clenched teeth. "You've been lying to yourself this whole time. I don't need to make you crazy—you already were, you know it."

"That's not true."

"Who cut you off? No one made you throw your phone in the fucking lake."

She has no answer to that. Cold anger lashes her; so he was watching her then, too. Or heard her mention it to Ellis. No part of her life has been her own for all this time.

She bends and picks up the shears; the handles are slick but she manages. Low, definitely trembling now, she asks the real question under all the rest.

"Are you infected?"

He barks a sickening laugh. "Are you?"

"Of fucking course I'm not."

"Are you sure?"

"Yes, I'm alive."

"So am I," he grates, "and you're still asking me. So how sure are you? Maybe we both are." He dissolves for a few seconds into a fit of wet coughing. "Maybe everyone is."

"Did it mutate?" She manages to wrestle in a breath. "Have the rules changed?"

"No one ever knew the rules. We were always only guessing." He lifts his head, and it's as if he can see her through the cloth. Maybe he can. Maybe it slipped a bit in his thrashing. "All the times you maybe got exposed and never knew. All the things you forgot."

"I never did the shit people do when they get infected," she whispers. "I never hurt anyone. Not before now."

He grins. His teeth are smeared with fresh blood. "Didn't you? Riley." His voice drops, hardens. "I need you to look now. Okay? I need you to take a really good, long look."

Footstep. She whirls, jerking the shears up, and there, standing in the kitchen doorway and backlit by warm setting sunlight, is a woman in a pair of dirty pink pajamas, a dirty bathrobe, brown hair a mess coming loose from its elastic tie, raw pits of nothing where her eyes should be. She raises her left hand and opens it, and they're resting in her blood-streaked palm, still wet, still alight with terrible awareness, staring at her.

"You wanted them, honey," her mother says gently. "You cut them out, but you never took them with you. So I brought them for you. Here." She proffers the eyes, swaying, smiling. Smiling the way she always did when Riley was scared or upset and in need of comfort, clinging and gazing into her eyes in search of reassurance. "It's okay. You can have them now."

"I didn't," Riley breathes. Never mind that this isn't possible. Never mind that her mother is miles away and years dead. "You—you did it, I found you after. I would have stopped you."

Behind her, the man is laughing and laughing.

"Oh, sweetheart." Her mother shakes her head. "No. Look."

The shadows beneath the trees. The shadows of her mother's house, every curtain drawn. The smell of musty closeness and a hint of decay. Picking her way across rocks and fallen branches, across trash and piles of unwashed clothes, bending to run her fingers over a scatter of shattered glass, picking up a long shard of it and turning it, watching it glisten in the dimness. A black feathered body hurtling through the air, a hunched shape bursting out of the dark and flying at her, grasping and gibbering—it's over, it's all over, no one can do anything, they're all going to die, they're all going to go mad and bleed and die.

One accusing eye staring at her, piercing through her to her soft unprotected center. Did she see it, then? Only a glimpse? Did it happen in that moment of chaos? Did it get inside her and break her and crack her open, and were they all wrong about it, and she's been carrying it around inside her since then?

Awkwardly straddling the body under her, bent and spattered with blood, the metallic reek of it, the scissors clutched in one hand.

The shears.

She rocks back a little, encounters the strange feeling of bent knees against her back. Some kind of edge. Looks down, blinking; the gashes across his throat, blood still pumping weakly from them but more sluggish by the second, his slit cheek and the pink-yellow edges of his teeth, his ear dangling absurdly from a thin strip of sinew, blindfold half pulled away and a churned reddish pulp where his left eye should be.

She cocks her head, considering this picture.

Wondering if this is a kind of freedom.

"Riley."

She turns. She still has the shears. If it's her mother, she's going to go at her. She's not going to put up with this any longer. Maybe ghosts can be hurt, and maybe they can't; she's going to establish the truth either way.

Ellis is standing where her mother was. And it's instinct now, has been for a long time, but even instinct isn't completely reliable. Does she see Ellis's eyes before she averts her own? Did she see the shell-shocked horror in them, or is she merely imagining it?

Does it matter now?

"Oh my God," Ellis whispers. "Oh my God, what the *fuck*, Riley, what the fuck did you *do*?"

36

She'll kill Ellis. That's all. She killed the man, she'll kill Ellis, and it won't be pretty or fun, but then she'll be safe. No one else will come. She'll make it work the way she always has. It'll be okay.

Maybe she can kill Ellis but keep Ellis here with her for a while. Maybe she can look in total safety into dead eyes. Or maybe, again, that stopped mattering a long time ago.

"I stopped him. He was trying to drive me insane," she says. She climbs off the man's body, shifting the shears in her grip. Hard to make that grip secure. She's covered in blood now, alternately slippery and tacky. "Like you." She points the shears at Ellis. "You, too. I never should have trusted you."

"He was—Fucking Christ, Riley, what are you *talking* about?" Ellis isn't backing away, isn't running, and also isn't coming closer. Ellis is standing as if rooted to the floor, absolutely still, hands half-raised as if preparing to fend Riley off but otherwise giving no indication that there's any threat here. It's bizarre. "Didn't you *hear* him?"

"Oh, I heard him. He told me enough." She's not angry anymore. More than anything else, she's tired, more than tired; this all sucks so much. For a while, it was so close to being good. "He told me he was working with you. Going after me. Didn't tell me why, but—"

"Working with—Riley, he had a car accident out on the fucking road, he needed *help*. He was screaming that he needed help, him and his daughter. He has a fucking *kid*. Oh, Jesus, he has a kid." Hands rising farther, clutching the side of Ellis's head. Finally Ellis is moving, not forward or back but shaking. Voice, muscles, everything, and for the first time, Riley feels the ugly little skittering legs of doubt moving across her scalp.

"Why are you here?" she breathes.

"I was worried, I was coming to find you, I heard him. I thought there was trouble. I didn't . . ." Ellis trails off, half falls against the doorframe, sinks. "Riley. Did you—did you look in his eyes?"

Riley doesn't answer. This could be acting. This could be the ultimate play, the ultimate trump card. Make her think she had no reason to do what she did. Make her think it was all a hideous mistake. She did go crazy. She was always crazy.

No. She heard what she heard.

"I didn't," she says softly. Then: "He said it didn't matter."

"Riley. I need you to put the scissors down." But Ellis isn't saying it with any particular conviction, only stunned flatness. "Okay? Can you do that for me?"

"I can't trust you."

A long moment of silence. Then Ellis murmurs, "No. No, I guess you can't."

Nothing happens for a while after that. Ellis sits fully against the doorframe, knees drawing up, and Riley lowers herself to sit on her heels, shears in her lap. She thought she would know what to do now. She thought everything would be clear after this. But she's working it over in her head, turning it this way and that, and in one version of this scenario, it's true and there's a kid out on the road somewhere, maybe trapped in a wrecked car, maybe in trouble, maybe hurt, maybe worse, and she just murdered a man who came looking for help and instead found a crazy woman with a pair of kitchen shears.

And in another version, there are two people who are crazy, who have been tormenting her for no reason at all, because she's crazy, too, everyone is crazy, everyone is infected, there never were any rules, and the world out there is nothing more or less than a sea of insanity from which she was never going to be able to escape.

"I think maybe I cut my mom's eyes out," she says finally. "I think maybe I got infected. I don't know. I can't remember." She raises a hand to the side of her head, feels there as though she might be able to detect some defect, some clue as to what's gone so terribly wrong. "I might be really fucked up, Ellis."

"You're not dead," Ellis says, tone like a stretch of featureless hardpan. "People get infected, they die."

"What if some people don't? What if we were wrong about what the rules are?" Riley takes a shaky breath. "How would we know? How would we know that? How could we ever be sure?"

"I don't know," Ellis says heavily after a moment. Then: "I don't know anything."

Riley is quiet. There doesn't seem to be anything to say to that. The man's body is getting cold. The blood is no longer flowing. The sun is going down, and the shadows are creeping in from the corners, extending long spidery fingers toward them both.

"There's a way to know one thing," she says presently. It comes to her all at once, blessedly simple, and she grabs for it with pathetic gratitude even as she quails and turns away from it. Because once she knows, she can't unknow it, and she'll have to live with it.

"What?"

"We go to the road." Riley exhales and begins to rise. She feels so much steadier with a task at hand, however terrifying its potential implications. "And I'll look. I'll see if he was telling the truth."

37

It feels oddly inappropriate to leave the man lying in the kitchen. In the end, Riley fetches a blanket from the living room and tosses it over him. She leaves the shears on the counter. She could bring them, she might still need to defend herself, but she realizes, somewhere between the living room and the kitchen, that she doesn't care anymore. If Ellis wants to attack her, let Ellis do that. It doesn't matter.

It would at least be some other kind of certainty, and some other kind of ending.

They walk in dense silence, Ellis slightly in front, moving wearily, head down. This feels, Riley thinks, a little like what she imagines walking the final stretch of death row to the execution chamber must feel like. She can't imagine a future beyond whatever they find out there. Whatever is or isn't there, she can't imagine what she might do in the moments and hours and days after. There's a body on her kitchen floor. There's blood everywhere, and all over her, stiffening her clothes and itching on her skin as it dries to a crusted scale. There's her food, which will run out. There's her store of other supplies, which will run out as well. She's been on borrowed time for years. She's cut off. She's alone.

Twilight is gathering itself over them as they reach the road. Riley looks left, right, sees nothing but the trees and the narrow ribbon of pavement snaking through them, and her gut lurches, and for an instant, she's sure she's going to vomit all over her shoes.

Ellis doesn't attack her. Only sighs and turns left. "Let's walk a little."

So they do.

About half a mile, perhaps, in one direction. They turn and backtrack, and a little farther in the other direction, they find the car.

An old blue station wagon. It's difficult to discern, just looking at it, how the accident happened, but there's no ambiguity about the state of the car itself. The driver's side is almost entirely intact, but the passenger's side is caved in, crumpled against a massive pine. A branch as thick as Riley's arm has speared through the windshield, the latter nothing more than a cascade of glittering fragments across the seats and the hood.

Glimpse of a small form in the passenger seat, only partially visible behind the branch. Riley turns away and bends over her knees, breathing. Breathing.

Crows fluttering and calling in the treetops, perching in a cold black audience on the telephone wire across the road.

Ellis pushes past her. "I'll look."

A few moments. Riley isn't sure how long. Her legs fold in a slow crumple, and she sits down on the pavement, staring at her bloody hands. The crows observe her in silence. They know. They've been watching her for a long time, evaluating, taking her measure, and now they're sitting in judgment. She remembers reading somewhere: Crows are said to escort the souls of the dead to the afterlife. Crows gather on battlefields, tending to the corpses. Crows are the ominous messengers of merciless gods.

A flock of crows is a murder.

Scuffle of a boot behind her, and Ellis's presence, solid as the pine. Riley wants so much to lean back into it.

"She's dead." Ellis pauses. "I think she's been dead for a while. She was hurt real bad. There might not have been much anyone could have done anyway."

Riley makes a sound that isn't quite a laugh. "Are you trying to make me feel better?"

"No," Ellis says simply.

"Okay."

Nothing. It always comes back to nothing. The darkness deepens. Riley sits and Ellis stands, and one by one, the stars begin to emerge, cold and still. Riley gazes up at them, passes her tongue across her lips, tastes blood. Today she tortured and murdered a man who needed her help, who had the bad luck of coming to the house of a madwoman. But it was always a desperate risk, seeking to make contact with someone. He knew that. Anyone might be mad these days. Eventually, perhaps everyone will be.

Everyone is infected. Some of us just hide it better than others.

At last, Ellis releases a long breath and steps past her. "Let's take a walk."

38

Back to the lake.

Because there isn't really anywhere else to go. Because sooner or later, one ends up here, standing on the bank, standing on the line between one thing and another, one state and another, one world and one entirely different. Riley thinks back, boots sinking into the mud, and realizes that she's always come here when she didn't know where else to go. There was a reason why she came here to get rid of the phone, when she might have disposed of it in any number of more convenient ways. She was stepping across a line. She wasn't losing her grip so much as looking for a way to let go.

Ellis's bad luck to be here, then.

Riley gazes over the water. It's very still, glassy, blue black touching blue black, and across it, behind the tree line, the moon is rising heavy and golden. No other lights in the trees; the other houses are dark and lifeless.

The world could be infected, insane. The world could also be dead, except for the two of them. How would she know?

How could she ever be sure?

"What if we were wrong?" she asks quietly. Beside her, a tall and powerful shape in the periphery of her vision, Ellis is motionless and silent. "Like I said. What if I'm infected? What if I've been infected this whole time?"

"I don't know."

"I did terrible things." Riley looks at her hands again, the blood dried to black smears. She could go to the water to wash them, but for some reason, she shies away from the idea. It feels like trying to lie. "I did such terrible things, sick things. What kind of person *does* those things?"

Ellis draws a slow breath. "The kind of people we've always been."

Riley nods. She supposes that, whatever the facts of her own state, that much is extremely true.

"Shit." Ellis releases a rueful laugh. "I really did like you. I liked you a whole fucking lot."

She glances at Ellis. No features there, except for a vague outline. She still doesn't quite know what Ellis looks like. The picture is so painfully incomplete. She has bits and pieces, the semi-connected fragments of a body and a face, but she can't see the whole. If she's already infected, maybe she's safe. Maybe they both are. Maybe she could have turned around that day, closed the last of the distance, looked and touched and let their hands and their mouths do what they wanted, because nothing matters.

And if it killed them both, well, again. Nothing matters.

Might have even been worth it, to not be alone anymore. Who can say? Who could ever be sure?

"Don't you like me now?"

Her mouth pulls into what feels like a humorless, agonized smile as she says it. It's a bad joke. She's insane, and she's a murderer. She's not safe. No one could like her now.

But Ellis laughs again, and it's less rueful and more purely sad. "Yeah. I do. I shouldn't, it's crazy, but I do."

"You came out here to get away from people like me."

"Maybe. Maybe not. Maybe there never was a reason." The outline is vague, but Riley thinks she sees and hears a smile as agonized as her own.

"Ellis." She turns. Finally, she turns, reaches out with her bloody hands and finds a pair of strong arms that tighten under her touch but don't pull away. She steps closer, erases the last of that distance, and Ellis's body against hers is every bit as strong and solid as she always half-consciously imagined it would be, and she leans into the solidity, borne up by it, smelling sweat and exhaustion and the gray dusty nothing-smell of grief mingling with her blood and madness. Presses her lips lightly and almost experimentally against the straight line of a jaw.

She was looking for a way to let go.

A heavy sigh and the right turn, the right angle, and a mouth against her seeking one, motionless and then working roughly, hands against her waist and a warm, powerful tongue licking into her, and she moans and opens to it and it's crazy and nothing matters.

She's gasping when she finally pulls back, and it's easy and thoughtless as she focuses her eyes and looks. For a moment, there's still nothing but shadow, and then the moonlight touches them both and she sees. Sees Ellis's face and knows it, feels the last of her cracking open and the last lingering grip released.

Ellis's eyes are half-closed, turned away from her.

Ellis's swollen, bloodstained lips are trembling. Riley smiles, wide and utterly, wonderfully insane, cups Ellis's beautiful face with both hands.

Nothing matters. And we were all always already crazy, and sick, and nothing ever has.

"Ellis," she whispers. "Look."

ACKNOWLEDGMENTS

First and foremost, this story wouldn't have happened without Nightfire's kind invitation to write the much shorter story it grew out of. Kristin Temple editorially shepherded both that story and this one across the finish line, and was a joy to work with; I owe her enormous thanks for her aid in shaping this book into the nightmare (in a good way) it's become. Sincere gratitude is also due to Kelly Lonesome and the whole team at Nightfire, and to David Seidman and Russell Trakhtenberg for the gorgeous cover art and design.

Thanks so much to my agent, Connor Goldsmith, who has been with me through a fair amount of flailing angst both before and after we got this in the pipeline, and who has borne it with patience and practicality. I wish I could say the angsting is done now, but, well, I'm a writer, so probably not.

Additional thanks should go to my dear friends Jessica Finn and Alexandra Erin, who have been endlessly supportive through some pretty difficult times, who believed that I could write and that my writing was worth doing when I had doubts about both. The term "cheerleader" feels a bit glib here, but the truth is that I couldn't ask for better ones.

I should tip a hat to my parents, who essentially condemned me to be a storyteller, and in particular, my beloved mother, who is probably more responsible than anyone else in my early life for my abiding interest in the unsettling and macabre. She knows why.

Thanks also to Sadie, even though she is a cat and therefore—as far as I can determine—cannot read. Sadie, you are the best around.

Finally, endless appreciation and love to my husband, who reads my drafts and doesn't pull his punches, who sticks with me when I won't shut up about whatever idea happens to be chewing at the edges of my brain, who supplies comfort and sympathy when things get overwhelming, and who has—in more ways than I could articulate—basically made this book possible. Love you, Rob. I promise that at some point, before we're both dead, I will have a normal day. Maybe.

ABOUT THE AUTHOR

SUNNY MORAINE is a writer of science fiction, fantasy, horror, and generally weird stuff, with stories published in outlets such as *Tor.com, Clarkesworld, Strange Horizons, Nightmare,* and *Uncanny.* A refugee from academia and the possessor of a Ph.D. in sociology, Moraine also writes, narrates, and produces a serial horror drama podcast called *Gone* and served as a writer on the Realm fiction podcast series *The Shadow Files of Morgan Knox.* They live near Washington, D.C., in a house that may or may not be haunted, with their husband and two cats.

sunnymoraine.com
Twitter: @dynamicsymmetry
Instagram: @sunnymoraine